An Angel's Whisper

Ryan Keith Johnson

"Red Dragon Fantasy: Song Lyrics and Poetry"
Copy Right © 2019
All rights reserved.
Red and Blue Dragon Fantasy LLC. and Lightning Source.
Cover Design by Ryan Keith Johnson
Photo taken by Dan Grevas
Sales tax included.
ISBN: 978-1-7339815-0-7

Other books:

"The King's Retribution"
"Lion Ascend"
"What I Think About You: Song Lyrics and Poetry"
"The Temple of the Incubus"
"Red and Blue Dragon Fantasy Legacy Anthology
of Compositions and Short Short Stories"
"Blue Dragon Fantasy: Faded Memories and Short Stories"
"The Culminate Amethyst"
"Red Dragon Fantasy: Song Lyrics and Poetry "

"Is everything in place?" asked President Krans.

"Yes, we're ready to proceed," said Omar Ashad as he stood by the console ready to push the button and turn the knob to open the portal.

"Initiate the process," ordered the president of the United States.

"Wait!" said a black hooded figure. "We must do our Luciferian chant."

"Proceed to do the chants, but remember our president is in charge," said a suited Caucasian.

"It's not fair," yelled the Luciferian as he raised his right hand in front of his chest to reveal his long fingernails. "We've been in contact with our master for the last eighteen years. He will be displeased if he isn't given a warm welcome."

"It's not fair for you, but for the Illuminati it is always fair," said the well dressed man in the suit as another man stepped next to him who looked like his twin. "The Illuminati will be the first to meet with this alien race. It is our duty to have the newest technology for world domination."

President Krans stepped in between the two business men and the five Luciferians.

Ryan Keith Johnson

"Mr. Black, Mr. Gray there is more than enough room for everyone to share the power and technology that our new friends from the other dimension can offer us," said president Kran as he turned to his friend and said,"Vaja let it go."

"He's my master and I will only follow him," said Vaja as he took off his big hood to reveal his long black hair, brown eyes and clean shaven face. "I will kill for him and do his bidding."

Mr. Black looked at the President, "This is not a good idea."

"This will work," said President Kran. "If he is who he claims to be he'll be able to change the world. He'll be able to help create technologies that will be beyond the Russian and the Chinese capabilities"

"He is God," said Vaja.

Mr. Black gave Vaja a disturbed look as did Mr. Gray, "there is no God. Only confused people who don't know how to unlock their power."

"The Illuminati have kept secrets hidden for centuries from fools like you," said Mr. Gray.

"You'll have to forgive, Mr. Gray. He doesn't believe in magic spells," said Mr. Black.

President Krans looked at both parties and then at his general, "are we going to get along? Because I don't want to give the order to open the gate if we're not united under one leader."

There was a moment of silence and President Krans spoke up , "do we have a problem?"

"We'll see what Lucifer has to say when he gets here," said Vaja.

"Well, I need to make sure you're going to stand with me because I don't want to find out you're going to back stab me in the future," said the president.

"I'll stand under you," said Vaja. "But I won't promise you that my master will keep you around."

President Krans looked at his general, "General Hex give the order."

General Hex turned to Omar and waved a gesture with his finger to begin the process. The scientist turned his head behind the council and they pressed a series of buttons and turned the large knob. The end of the machine began to light up with white light and the end of it shot a white laser from the end of a satellite dish into the end of the room where it stopped just before a stone wall. There was a strange popping and humming noise as the fabric of air began to rip apart. The colors from the fabric being ripped apart was red and as it grew wider there was a vacuum of air that was pushing outward at about sixty miles an hour. There was a stale taste in the air that was like sulfur and burnt wood and the air was warm. Inside the portal, the people could see a glimpse of red skies and what looked like buildings in the distance.

After several minutes passed the portal was about ten feet in diameter and growing. When it got to twelve feet in circumference a large shadow emerged and when it got closer it stepped through. The president looked at the creature in shock and couldn't believe what he was looking at.

The ten foot archangel walked towards the president slowly. He was wearing a gold metal tunic around his waist and had white albino skin. He was beautiful and had what looked like tiny diamonds on his muscular body. In his right hand he held a gold scepter with precious stones. The top of it was shaped like a crown and it extended about a meter. His face was masculine with a strong ridged jaw bone, but no facial hair which made him feminine. His iris was a light blue and when he looked at the people responsible for letting him out he looked intimidating. The being looked like a giant body builder with a mullet of white hair that was just below his neck.

"Who released me and my followers?" said the being with a deep voice.

2

"I am the one that allowed it," answered the President of the United States. "What is your name?"

"I am Lord of Light, The Master, my children call me Lucifer. My Father calls me Satan."

"What do you want me to call you?" asked President Krans.

"That depends," began the angel. "Are you my child or are you the fool?"

"I am the President of the United States and theses people answer to me."

The angel looked at the little man with dis-trust at first, but as he walked over to the human he noticed the little man was scared of him, "Lord of Light will suffice for now. Tell me Mr. President, what type of title do you represent?"

"Well," began President Krans as he stammered. "I run a country, I tell people what to do and serve the public."

"No," said the angel with a deep gravel.

"What?" asked president Krans.

"You serve me now."

"But I released you from whatever it is you came from. You serve me," said President Krans.

"The Master doesn't serve anyone, it is my followers and my children that follow me."

"But I released you," said the president.

The angel ignored what he said and smiled as he kneeled down to the little man, "I offer you riches beyond your wildest dreams. If you serve me all you have to do is prove it."

"What do I get?"

"I don't know, what do you want?" asked the Master.

"I want to own this country and not have to have an election again," said President Krans.

"It is done, you will also receive jewels and precious stones." said the angel as he rose up from kneeling. "But before we get started you must worship me."

"I'm sorry, what did you say?" he asked.

"You heard what I said little man," replied the Master in a serious tone.

The president looked at General Hex, Vaja and Mr. Black. He then turned to the ten foot angel and opened his mouth as he stuttered.

"I want to know what I get out of this?"

"For a man who wants to rule this country you waste a lot of time. I already told you that you shall receive many jewels, gold and silver in your honor for being at my side," said the Master calmly with his voice, but his voice soon changed as it became loud and forceful as his expression became angry. "Now kneel before me, clasp your hands together and pray to me!"

The president felt his knees grow weak and he got down on one knee and clasped his hands together and began to pray.

"Oh great master, I welcome you in my life and hope for deliverance and peace while you are here."

"Say that you will do what I tell you and that your life belongs to me," said the Master and the president repeated what he was told.

"You will kill your wife and children in my honor."

The president stopped for a minute and looked at the Master in the eyes and could see how icy cold they were with death, but continued on with what he wanted.

"You give me your soul that once belonged to the Host of Heaven, to me, the Lord of Light," continued the Master and heard the president repeat what he said.

The Master smiled and looked at the president with ease and respect. President Krans looked up and was gestured by the Lord of Light to rise up. He rose up but felt like he lost a part of himself and that he was now under bondage.

Thousands of demons emerged out of the portal as did many with four legs; hell hounds, imps and other demonic creatures. The thousands of imp like demons flew around the cave in droves and some of them flew around The Lord of Light. Some of the demons were leathery and dragon like while others looked like smaller versions of the ten foot angel. They had pale colored skin, looked tired, their white feathery wings looked dirty as though they had fallen in a tar pit and hadn't been able to recover from it.

"Mr. President," said the Master.

"Yes sir," said President Krans.

"Prepare a speech, tell your countrymen you have found new life forms and that you're excited to invite them into your world to help with their endeavors."

"Yes sir," said the president as he was about to leave.

"Wait, take my best warrior, Master Scaven. He will protect you from harm. Master Scaven take Brehem and assemble an army."

"Yes sir," said the gargoyle like beast as he walked with the president and left the cave.

The Master looked at the scientist, "you were able to open up a hole to bring me through?"

Omar said nothing and looked scared. The Master walked towards them and the machine. "Build me an army of nephilims."

Rya stared at his laptop screen as he sat in deep thought. It was nine o'clock on a Saturday morning and he was in a writer's block. There was a song playing on the radio called "It's in my Dream That I See Her", that made him think of her. It was a happy and sad song. He took a breath and exhaled as he finished the sentence. He thought about Krissy and the time he had met her and wondered how she was doing right now. It had been many years since she left his life and he hoped that she was happy.

He prepared breakfast and cracked open some eggs and put it in the pan. He pulled out the ingredients for an omelette and some bacon strips he cooked yesterday.

He had been working on this novel for six months and it wasn't going anywhere. He began to have second thoughts about continuing it. Suddenly, he felt a vibration in the kitchen as though someone was walking near him. Rya turned around and to see it was Sarah.

"Oh it's you."

"Problems again?" she asked.

"No problems, just writer's block," he replied as he put all of his ingredients in the pan to make his omelette.

"Maybe you should take a break and go to the art fair down town, in Hustle."

"Yeah, that would help me unwind," Rya replied as he waited for a few minutes before flipping his omelette and let it cook some more. "Is there anything good to look at?"

"I don't know, you might find some inspiration," said Sarah.

Rya looked at her and started laughing, "yeah right."

"Then don't go," she replied. "You won't get very far in your work if you don't get inspiration."

"No you're right I should. I mean, I will," he replied. "But after I finish my breakfast."

Sarah looked at Rya with a peculiar look and then smiled, " I think you will like what you will find, but you should bring your laptop."

"You're not coming?"

"No I'm not, I have a meeting to attend, but I'll be back as soon as I can."

"Ok, well I'll see you later," replied Rya as he watched her disappear out of thin air.

Rya walked around the art fair to see the white tents with merchants inside that were selling everything from paintings, jewelry, food, and natural remedies. He took a closer look in the white tents to look at the art work. He enjoyed looking at the paintings and illustrations because it gave him plenty to think about. Suddenly, he came across a familiar face that nearly knocked the wind out of him. A woman who was bent down at the check out counter rose up with a large plastic bag to put over a painting for a customer. At first Rya thought that it was his guardian angel but then he noticed there were small differences in height and a slight change in body shape, but it was unbelievable.

"Sarah," he whispered to himself as he saw the woman who had long whitish blonde hair and blue eyes at the cash register.

She was busy helping an old lady and was wearing blue jeans, a blue t-shirt and a brown sports jacket. Rya walked over to the table and looked at her as she smiled when she made a sale on the illustration. He couldn't tell what it was because the lady who bought it turned away to leave and it was put in a giant bag. Rya turned his head to see the woman who looked like Sarah turn and smile at him.

"Hi, can I help you ?" she asked.

"No, I'm just looking," he stammered as he started looking at some of her art work and tried to relax. "You're really good."

"Thank you, I've been doing it since I was a teenager. I decided I wanted to be an artist when I graduated high school."

The sound of her voice was medium, a little bit emotional and confident. Rya could tell she wore her heart on her sleeve and grew up in a good home. Just by the sound of her voice, Rya knew she wasn't like his guardian angel Sarah who was more logical, less emotional and more strong willed.

"Right," smiled Rya as he looked at her. "What inspired you to create these wonderful pieces?"

"People inspire me," she answered while looking at him peculiarly.

"That's cool, what's your favorite medium?"

"For the most part I like to work in HB pencil, but I'm comfortable illustrating in ink. You look familiar, have we met somewhere?"

"My name is Rya," he replied as he held his hand out.

"Hi, I'm Sara," she shook his hand. "Now I remember you, aren't you that author that was in the newspaper a few weeks ago?"

"Yes," he answered.

"Oh my God," she laughed. "I would love to hear about your latest work."

"Great, why don't we meet at Coffee Today," he replied.

"Ok, how about eight o'clock," she smiled.

"That's fine."

Rya sat in a booth at the Coffee Today which was down the street. He was excited to see her and looked at his watch to see it was a few minutes after eight. Suddenly, the doors opened and there she was and Rya smiled.

She looked different and Rya saw that she was wearing a dress and make up. She smiled as she sat down at the booth and a few minutes later a waiter walked over to take their orders and then left

"How was your day?" asked Rya.

"It was good, I sold five more paintings," she replied just before the waiter returned with a cold coffee that had chocolate, crushed ice and whip cream.

"I'll be back with the appetizers," said the waiter before he left.

"So Rya, what is your last name?" asked Sara

"My last name is Adams," replied Rya as he suddenly heard a peculiar song the radio that kept repeating, it's in my dreams that I see her, and then he looked at her. She smiled at him and then laughed.

"What's so funny?" he asked.

"Nothing, it's just that you remind me of someone a long time ago."

"So what's your last name?"

"Adrienne."

"Are you enjoying yourself in Hustle?" he asked

"Yes, the people are friendly and they have nice places to go to."

"Where are you from?"

"New York City, my parents brought me there when I was a three. I'm was born in Boston."

"Do you have any brothers and sisters?" asked Rya.

"Yes I do, I have an older brother and sister and a younger sister and brother."

"Five kids? That's got to be rough?"

"No, not really, she laughed. "My father is the number two guy at Brothers Investments. He's in charge of liquidating companies that are out of business and selling the parts for money. The company buys companies and also works as an investment firm."

"That's cool, why didn't you work for your father?" he asked.

"Because I'm an artist, not a corporate executive. My older brother and sister are already working for them."

Rya looked into her eyes and then her mouth and felt the desire to kiss her. She was cute, beautiful and full of life. He watched her take a sip from her strawed ice coffee, her eyes were lowered to look at it and he took a drink from his ice coffee and soon the waiter came back with the appetizers of onion rings, chicken wings and cheese sticks.

"So tell me about your family? Where does your father work?" she asked

Rya hesitated as he ate some of his onion rings.

"He does work right?" she asked. "He's not a toilet bowl cleaner, is he?" she started laughing.

Rya started to chuckle, "no, my dad's name is Bill and he works as a manager for a company called TJ Supplies. It's a company that builds parts for manufacturing companies. They build parts for cranes, bicycles and motorcycles."

"That's nice," she replied with a smile. "Why didn't you get a job working there?"

"I did, but I quit after a couple years. My older brother works there and is a supervisor. I wanted to write and worked a couple of odd jobs until my first book came out."

"How many brothers do you have?" she asked.

"I have two, and I'm the middle child," smiled Rya.

"We're both middle children and we're both artists ," she laughed as she continued. "What about your mother, what does she do?"

"She was a stay at home mom, but decided to get into an MLM company called "Fragrances and Smiles", that sells soaps and candles."

Rya looked at Sara and could feel an attraction from her. He knew by the look in her eyes that she was in love with him and they had just scratched the surface.

Suddenly, they were interrupted by the news from the TV that was hanging on the wall near them. It was the President of the United States who announced that they had made a break through in science and uncovered another dimension. They had met a group of beings that wanted peace with them and to help the people of America.

"What is it?" asked Sara after she looked at the television and then back at Rya.

"You ever get the feeling that something bad is about to happen?" asked Rya as he turned his eyes from the TV back to her.

"Sometimes, when I fall asleep I have nightmares I'm falling into darkness," she said looking scared. "Sometimes I'm on the edge of a cliff and I can't get away from it."

Rya slowly and gently took her hand and said, "then you wake up from those nightmares, but not the ones that are in the waking state."

They talked until it was time for the coffee shop to close and Rya walked with her to her motel room. She turned around to look at him and smiled before he kissed her. Rya could feel her dried firm lips and the massage of her mouth and tongue with his. It lasted for a few minutes, but for Rya it felt like an eternity. When it was over she looked at him and smiled.

"Good night," she whispered.

Rya felt his heart skip a couple of beats as he caught his breath and whispered back, "good night."

The next day Rya woke up with the song, It's in my Dreams That I See Her, in his head, and the only thing that was on his mind was seeing Sara again. After cleaning up and changing his clothes he left to go down to the art show to visit her.

"Hi," he said as soon as he saw her and she immediately smiled.

"You're back again," she laughed.

"I wanted to see you."

"Well I'm at work. I can't really talk."

"Can I help?" he asked as he noticed the way she looked at him, which was the same look at the coffee shop. "I would like to keep you company."

"Ok."

Rya worked with Sara through the week and when she was finished with her shift at eight o'clock they walked down to the docks by the river and talked about their goals. She listened to him talk about his next book and held his hand as they laughed together about movies they had seen that were funny. They also talked about how the world has changed and how harmful it was for families.

The time they were apart, Rya found a boost in creativity of things he never considered and an abundance of energy as he was able to continue typing none stop for hours. It seemed unbelievable as to how long and quickly he was able to type the information onto the keyboard.

When the carnival closed, they spent Saturday together at Crystal Cave and walked around the shops of Hustle, looking at nick knacks and souvenirs. He looked at her and she looked at him and they secretly kissed in the aisle of the stores until the store manager caught them and gave them a cough with the gesture to leave. They started laughing and they walked out the door. When they got back to her motel room they kissed outside her door from dusk to midnight and then it started to rain.

"Oh shit," said Rya as he looked around.

"Come inside," she whispered as she opened the door and they walked in where it was dry and warm.

Rya stared at the computer screen with a pen in his mouth. He was having a writer's block and could only think of the last night with Sara and the long night they spent together. He couldn't forget about her and it kept him from focusing. He remembered when he fell in love with Krissy and she left him in a depression because she was off to be a career girl and didn't want him.

The writer logged off his computer, took out his USB and put the lap top in his back pack. As of now he had made up his mind to see her and tell her to stay with him. He put on his jean jacket and left after he locked the door. As he walked to the door to leave the building. He heard a loud commotion outside on the streets. He could hear the sound of gunfire, screaming, yelling, growling and car tires squealing as well as the sound of crashes into buildings. Rya felt the hair on the back of his neck raise up as he opened the door.

There was a riot outside and looting. There were army men dressed in black that wore what looked like kevlar and rubber body armor with a mark of a bird with its wings spread open and what looked like wheat crossed into each other at the stem forming a 'V'.

Rya quickly looked up to see two imp like demons attack him, but he pushed them aside and made a run for it down the street. The police with Glock 22 and PTR 91 Semi Auto Rifles fired at the imp creatures and the men that bare the marks on their arms also carried machine guns turned and fired at the police. Two large dogs with red fur and glowing red eyes attacked and killed the injured cops. They looked at Rya and growled but feasted on the corpse. Rya was horrified when he looked up to see the imp demons flying around the top of his apartment like swarms of birds. The shoot out continued and one cop after the other fell to the ground until numerous seven to eight foot creatures glided down to the ground. Some of them looking like angels but with a gray color in their skin and wings. They weren't white and beautiful like Sarah and Sarrjel. Then the demons glided down, looking like gargoyles with lavender skin red and black hair and red eyes. Some of them had yellow or orange eyes and wore a leather tunic with a breast plate armor similar to Rome and metal guards to protect their limbs. The female demons wore similar clothes, but were more sexual as human females are. The name Nation United appeared on black army trucks and Jeeps with the same logo he saw from the soldier's arm. It was frightening and Rya didn't know what to do. Those that resisted were shot dead and the police retreated as they fired their guns. The civilians that were running away were shot by a passing predator drone with a big machine gun and ambushed by demons to be taken prisoner. Rya reached the corner of a building that was ten blocks down the street from where he ran. He creeped by the edge of the building and felt his heart race. He took a step back as soon as he saw two men in body armor wearing masks. They charged after him and he ran as fast as he could to get away.

"Hey, Stop!" yelled the first soldier as he drew his hand gun.

Rya heard a loud flapping noise that sounded like wings and peeked around the corner of the dumpster and saw a demon standing next to the two men. The two men saluted, "hail Ravens and the Nations United."

"What are you doing," said the demon in a very deep voice.

"We're chasing a civilian and he's hiding here," said the first soldier.

Rya took a deep breath while looking scared as they walked closer to him. He could see the demons' leathery feet with the soldier's boots. The garbage cans were moved aside and Rya was discovered.

"Why were you running away?" asked the first soldier.

"What's your identification number?" asked the second soldier.

"He doesn't have one," said the demon.

"Let's take him to camp twelve," continued the first soldier.

Then suddenly, he saw something fly behind them that was white and had wings. It grew brighter as it drew closer and it kicked the demon ten feet along the ground into the dead end and attacked the two men by temporarily blinding them and knocked them down. The two orbs of light hovered two feet in the air before materializing and revealed themselves wearing silver and leather armor. The soldiers came to and fired their machine guns at the angels. The bullets struck them and were deflected by the armor, but their faces were hit. They were skewed by the bullets that had struck them in the face and bounced off, but were unharmed. The angels looked like they were in pain and began crying, but after a minute they rose back up from being heaved over in agony.

Light emerged from their bodies and minutes later their wounds healed heir armor disappeared to reveal what looked like night gowns over their skin. They looked at the soldiers who fired at them and gave them an angry look. The soldiers looked scared and Sarrjel pulled out her sword and pointed at them and spoke in tongues as a burst of fire struck them, turning them into white statues made of salt. Sarrjel slid her sword back in its sheath.

The demon rose up from the ground and snarled at the angels. His yellow, gargoyle eyes began to close part way as he sneered. He was a masculine demon that was eight feet tall, lavender colored skin, with moderate armor, black claws, long oily black hair that stretched past his shoulders and when he smiled his fangs could be seen.

"It's good to see you. Master Scaven and Angel Hunter Malicious are looking for you."

"What do you want Brehem?" commanded Sarrjel.

"We want you," began Brehem with a wicked smile. "We want Rya and the militias. We want to make the world a better place, but we need people and angels who will conform to our leader's laws."

"Well you can't have him," ordered Sarrjel. "He belongs with us, just as good men of this country belong to Him and we would rather die than serve your leader," declared Sarrjel as she looked at Sarah with confidence.

Sarrjel pulled out her sword which had a black handle with silver stripes. There was a diamond on the bottom of the handle. The handle had two guards that also held diamonds on the blade. There was an engraving of the queen of the angel's face. The blade was silver with a strange white color. Sarrjel called her sword the Sword of Righteousness.

"Oh come on," said Brehem. "You can't beat me and there's no escape. Give in to me and I promise you will be spared."

"The only adventure that will lead you next will be your head lying on the ground several feet from your body!" said Sarah.

"I never introduced you to my personal friend of mine. This is the Blood of Revenge and it has never lost a match," answered the demon as he pulled out his sword

"There is always a first time for everything," said Sarah.

"This is my friend, the Sword of Righteousness," said Sarrjel.

Brehem began to laugh and swung his sword. It looked like an ordinary sword but was made of gold with an engraving of a demon on the front with its wings spread out extending up the blade. He moved it slowly in front of him and then quickly around his shoulders. The demon opened his bat like wings and charged as he unleashed a roar. Sarrjel charged and caught every swing of Brehem's sword with hers. She adapted to his strikes and her dexterity felt a pinch from the strong blows of his blade.

Sarah took Rya's hand and they moved out of the way from the attack. They both watched the guardian angel and the demon fight viciously. Sarrjel looked like she was going to need help and was barely able to keep up with the speed that was being unleashed.

"Sarah you better help her," said Rya.

"Are you sure?"

"I'll be fine, right now she needs your help."

Sarah nodded and opened up her wings as she flew up in the air while the demon continued to swing his sword. Sarah swooped down behind Brehem and quickly jumped on his back and putt her arm around the demon's throat and chocked him while covering his eyes. The demon growled as he dropped his sword to reach for Sarah but couldn't get a good grip. Her white wings opened up like a bird as she continued to squeeze the demon's throat.

"Now!" yelled Sarah as she watched her sister nod and charge with her sword.

The demon let out a roar in pain as Sarrjel stabbed him in the chest and moved out of the way quickly to avoid getting punched in the face. Brehem grabbed Sarah's arm with his hand and swung her over his head. The demon then held her up with both hands and was choking her. Sarah started coughing as she was slammed against the brick wall. Sarah was knocked out and Brehem, who thought he had killed her, threw her lifeless body behind him like a rag doll at the end of the alley.

Brehem grabbed Sarrjel by the throat simultaneous as he discarded Sarah and pulled her sword from her hand throwing it aside as he picked her up a few feet from the ground. Sarrjel began coughing as she felt his tight grip around her and watched the demon reveal a sneer. Suddenly, there was a bright light behind Brehem and a blade cut into his arms and abdomen. Sarrjel fell to the ground and the angels watched the demon scream in pain and fly away in retreat.
Sarah extended her hand to Sarrjel and they both saw that they were bruised and a little bit bleeding, but they were alive. They turned to Rya who was watching the battle the whole time and was happy they won. He watched Sarrjel breathe deeply as she got up with Sarah's help.

"I never encountered a demon that powerful before," said Sarrjel.
"Do you think our power is diminishing?" asked Sarah.
"I don't know, but we need to keep moving," replied Sarrjel.

The angels turned their head to Rya who was looking behind them, towards the dead end area. They saw a man in camouflage clothes with a five o'clock shadow who wore a dark green helmet. He was a white, five foot nine with an M-16 in his arm and he wore an army vest with grenades tied around his shoulders. He looked like he was in his early forties with touch of gray hair on both sides of his head.
He pulled his M-16 at the angels, "get the hell away from him!"

The angels looked at him disgruntled as they took a step back and rose their hands up. Sarah looked at Sarrjel and then at Rya who was scared about what was going to happen next.
"Come with me, I'm the leader of a militia group and we are picking up civilians and anyone else that we can save from this hell."
"But that is why we are here," said Sarah as she lowered her hands. "If you would just give us a chance to explain."
"You are the reason we're in this shit, so back off!" yelled the man and he watched Sarah raise her hands back up.
"Come on, let's go!"
"Wait, who are you?"
"I'm Joe and I'm part of the United States Militia for Wisconsin. We're part of the Black Hawk Group Special Forces.
"That's why we're here?" said Sarrjel.
"We can help!" said Sarah as she continued. "Let us help."
"I'm not leaving without them, they're here to protect me," said Rya.

Joe lowered his gun and shook his head, "I hope you know what your doing. Those creatures are part of this shit and civil unrest that is going on right now."

Sarrjel picked up her sword and joined Sarah to follow Joe up the wall of the alley. Rya climbed up the rope and the angels flew to the roof where Joe was. Joe looked at the angels who smiled at him, but ignored them when Rya pulled himself up on the rope to the top of the building.

They looked around to see smoke in the sky and heard explosions in the distance of the state of Minnesota that could be described as demolition bombs. They ran as fast as they could through an obstacle of hangers, generators and heat ex-changers that were on the roof of building.

Rya followed Joe to the edge of the building to see him climb down with a tied rope to a chimney and Rya followed after seeing an Army Jeep down below in an open ally. Once Joe and Rya made it down to the bottom of the rope. Rya looked up to see his two angels stay where they were and looked at him. Sarrjel put her hand in front of Sarah's chest to gesture her to wait. Rya turned to look at Joe who gestured Rya with his hand to get in the Jeep and when he did Joe stepped on the gas. Rya turned around to look at his guardian angels and was wondering why they were staying behind. He then turned around to look at Joe.

"Where are we going?"

"Its' alright, we're going to our training camp. It's a few miles away in the sticks."

They continued to drive past the enemy soldiers who were shooting at the Jeep and the bullet proof glass. Joe shot at them back with his pistol and threw hand grenades, over the glass, at the attackers before eluding them. They escaped by turning off on other streets and sped faster, sometimes through small residential neighborhoods and through personal property to avoid the mobs of people and attackers.

The group finally made it in the clear and were out of the of the township. They suddenly took a turn down a ditch and into a trail. They were stopped by a dozen well armed men who recognized Joe and let him pass with a secret hand gesture. They continued to drive through the forest for about a mile until they were at a camp. There were tents, RV's and a group of people dressed in camouflage. They were armed with varies rifles, shot guns and other weapons.

Joe got out of his Jeep as Rya did and the group of resistant fighters walked towards them. Five German Shepherds ran up to Rya and began sniffing him. One of the dogs did a light gruff and growled.

"At ease," commanded Joe to the dogs. "There, there now."

One of the masked militias walked towards them and whistled for the dogs to draw back. He uncovered his face and stood in front of Joe about a foot. The man took off his helmet and saluted. He was clean shaven with a tan colored skin and had a crew cut. He stood a few inches taller than Joe and looked like he was in his late twenties or early thirties. He wore full camouflage shirt, pants and jacket and had a belt that holstered his pistol. On the other side was a hunting knife that was nearly a foot long and it was holstered as well.

He replied with a deep voice, "we have everything in order and sent messengers to other militia units across the state, informing them of our position and to stand by."

"Excellent," began Joe with a nod. "This is Rya, I found him while the city was burning by our enemies and the creatures. We could use another hand."

"Nice to meet you, my name is Grant White and we call ourselves The Zion Outpost," said Grant as he shook Rya's hand and then looked at Joe. "Sir, what are we dealing with?"

"We don't know. These creatures are helping our enemies pick us off one by one and two of the creatures were with Rya. They can also disguise themselves to look angelic, like the things you see in church," said Joe.

"I thought you said you were part of the Black Hawk Group," said Rya.

"We are an extension of that group," said Joe.

"The Black Hawk Group is part of Black Water and Special Forces with the CIA. We are independent."

"How did these creatures get here?" asked Grant. "There has to be a logical reason why they are here and how they have remained hidden for so long."

"Well there is the bible. I thought it was just a fairy tale written by crazy old men in a cave." said Joe. "I guess that shows how much I know."

"So everything is real?" asked Grant.

"I don't know," answered Joe.

"Not everything you see is evil," said Rya.

Suddenly, Grant grabbed his gun as Joe heard the dogs barking and saw the two angels flying overhead, "speak of the devil."

Sarrjel and Sarah were flying overhead at about two-hundred feet and glided down quickly feet first while their wings were spread open. They landed on the ground slowly and the militia pointed their weapons at them. The five German Shepherds ran towards the angels and started to growl, but then stopped. They began to whine and cry as Sarah reached out to touch the leader of the pack. The leading German Shepherd was Shadow and he had blue eyes. He walked towards Sarah and sat down in front of her while she pet him. Then all the dogs walked up panting and licking both of the angels' hands. The angels looked around at the humans in fear when suddenly Rya ran in front of them.

"What are you doing?" exclaimed Rya. "These are my friends!"

"Stand down!" yelled Joe as he signaled his militia to lower their weapons.

"Who are these creatures?" yelled a man in his mask. "We've dealt with these monsters before, how can we trust them?"

"We give you our word that we're not here for deceit!" commanded Sarrjel

"We've come to help you in your fight!" declared Sarah.

"Yeah right, you bunch of demons!" yelled a woman.

"She's telling you the truth, we've come to help. We know what's happening and want to lead you to salvation," declared Sarrjel.

"Yeah, right," yelled a young black man in his mid twenties. "We living in the sticks, until you ogres come breaking down my door while I watch cable with microwave dinner!"

"We know," assured Sarah. "It's only going to get worse. Jesus wants us to bring you together and deliver you to salvation--"

"I don't know Jesus and neither do you, bitch!" said the black man. "You trying to deceive us and get us killed!"

"Deputy, that's enough," said Joe as he looked at the other militias before continuing. "All friends of Rya's are friends of ours in our fight to restore this nation," declared Joe as he looked at his country men. "And I'll have words with anybody who continues to abuse our guests simply by the way they look!"

The militia lowered their rifles, shot guns, AK 47s, AR 15 Rifles and DPMS G2 Compact hunter Semi Auto Rifle. 308. The angels felt relief and took a deep breath.

The rest of the militia unraveled their masks and walked up to Rya to shake hands. They introduced themselves as Jason, Irina, Barry, George, Jeremy, Brenda, Dallas, Deputy and there were many others that Rya couldn't keep track of, but some of them took a step back from introduction because of the affiliations that the newcomer had with the angels. The militia were a motley crew of sorts that consisted of police officers, fire men, National Guard, Marines, bankers, carpenters, secretaries, doctors and business managers. The angels walked over to Rya to comfort him. Rya looked at Sarah who looked at him with assurance by giving him a nod.

"I'm glad you're here," he said. "In this time of despair I can't think of anyone I would want by my side than you two."

"Thank you, but we're not out of the woods yet," said Sarrjel.

"Rya, I want you to come with me," said Joe as he looked at him and the angels.
"You two can come as well."

"I don't understand, what are we going to talk about?" asked Rya.

"It's a meeting that we have and all the militia members are invited to know what our plan is," said Joe.

Rya looked at Grant who nodded his head slowly to show that he wanted to include him in the loop. Rya followed Joe and Grant into a large tent with a big table inside. Sarah and Sarrjel were behind Rya and sensed hostility from the members of the militia. The tent was huge with a large table that was about twenty feet in length and twelve feet in width. It had a strange map and model of all the cities and lands of Wisconsin and Minnesota. There were, what looked like small model cities or towns that had metal tokens. Each token was a different color and there were safety pins with various colored flags.

Joe took off his helmet and Grant waited patiently for the chatter and comments from the militias to be silent. Grant raised his hand up to show his countrymen it was time for the meeting to start. After the last chatter ceased the second in command nodded to Joe.

"Here we are, several miles from Hustle in the farm country, near the cheese factory and the Ravens have seized control of all major cities and large towns," said Joe.

"I heard on the CB that the Raven's have been rounding people up and putting them in internment camps," said Grant.

"Any ideas of what they're doing?" asked Dallas.

"Not a clue," replied Grant.

"They're probably re-education camps," said Deputy with a smile. "Time to go to school."

"I also heard on the CB that there have been attacks on preppers, stragglers and the lone wolves who want to do it alone. Those who have tried to bug out have ended up stuck on the streets or in their home in a gun fight with the Ravens and military police and those alien creatures," said Grant as he looked at Sarrjel.

"It's ok," began Sarrjel. "You can call them fallen angels."

"Yeah, ok fallen angels," said Grant with his head down and then he raised it up to look at Sarrjel with a light smile.

"What about the children?" asked Irina.

"We don't know what happened to the children," said Joe.

"What happened? How did this happen?" asked Rya.

"Don't know, it's nothing we did," began Joe. "We elected the wrong people and other people were up to no good. The question is, what do we do now?"

"The president said that they found a bunch of aliens in a cave in Nevada," said Brenda as she continued. "It was all over the news yesterday."

"So the big man is responsible for all this? How typical," said Deputy.

"It probably has, but we haven't heard everything," said Joe.

"If this is happening all over. Why is there not a big revolt?" asked Diamond Back Daryl.

"Man isn't perfect and will never be perfect," said Sarah.

"And I suppose you're perfect," said Joe.

Sarah looked at Joe, "no I am not."

"Where did the demons come from?" asked Barry. "I mean why didn't we see them come sooner in Earth's history or even the last couple of days?"

"I think I can explain," said Sarrjel.

"I'm all ears," said Joe.

"Demons, fallens, super beasts, imps, dragon cats, hell hounds and Satan were locked away in a what we call a Hole. It's a prison for these angels that don't want to follow our ways. The problem is that the demons can still branch out from astral projection and control human beings from committing to their goals, they're natural growth. Somehow your human counter parts, who are the Ravens must have breached the Hole and allowed them to escape from the the meta physical boundaries of the dimensional rift into what you humans call the physical, the human world," said Sarrjel as she looked at Joe and Grant and then the rest of the militia. "We were sent as guardians for Rya to bring him to salvation and into the world of eternity, which is a skin deep from this world."

"If that's true, then where are our guardian angels?" asked Barry.

"Our Father, Host of Heaven called us back to allow judgment to fall on the remain who shall bare witness to the Rapture. We came back to bring Rya and anyone else we find to salvation, away from the wicked."

"I don't understand," said Irina. "Why send two angels? Why not send hundreds or thousands?"

"Is this some kind of Alice in Wonderland bull-shit?" asked George.

"If this is such an important thing for you then why are there only two of you?" asked Joe. "Two guardian angels against an army of demons plus the Ravens isn't smart thinking," he continued.

"It's part of His plan," said Sarrjel. "We were sent to bring a small group of humans that would trust in His judgment and ours."

"What is the other world and what is a skin deep from this world?" asked Grant.

"This world isn't real," began Sarrjel slowly. "It's a training ground, to test you, to give you new ideas to take with you for what you left behind. It is new thinking."

"New thinking? What is that shit from? The book 1984?" asked Deputy.

"Left behind? Does that mean re-incarnation?" asked Cab.

Sarrjel didn't answer, "there is so much you don't understand."

"If things are so perfect in your world and we already lived there then why the fuck would we want to leave and live in this shit hole in the first place?" asked Deputy.

"I will say no more," said Sarrjel. "If you read the bible you will get your answers. The scribes worked hard to make the answers available, even as corruption in the church has removed the wisdom of what Jesus has taught, those that listen and open their arms shall receive. The fruits of the wisdom shall grow plentiful, but for those that keep their hands crossed and their head down the seeds shall not grow and the future shall be lost."

"So for me to understand this magical world I need to go to a church and read a bible?" said Deputy as he started laughing.

"Knock it off," said Joe

"You cross your arms and spite the teachings of your great lord and so you shall receive nothing, but if you open your arms wide you shall be plentiful and live in abundance. There you will open your eyes and see the Kingdom of God," declared Sarrjel as she felt a huge weight of silence that lasted for minutes.

"Ok, well, back to what we were talking about," began Joe. "How are we doing on supplies?"

"Supplies are good," said Grant. "We've been planting gardens and trying to barter with farmers to get some live stock, but we haven't been successful. We've got enough canned foods as well as perishable foods to last two years maybe three."

"How are we doing on fuel?" asked Joe.

"We were able to get twenty medium propane tanks and ten large tanks. We have about 50 gallons of gasoline in five gallon jugs for our trucks and campers. We have about twenty gallons of premium to power our motorcycles and dirt bikes, our electric fat bikes have been a big help, but they rely on the batteries. If the batteries go dead then it will make it difficult to peddle in the outback, over hills."

"Excellent work," said Joe as he continued. "The Raven Army is moving populations to centers. These centers are huge and house thousands of people. I was there, myself, to watch with my binoculars. A contact of mine, who escaped, told me what went on inside."

"What is that?" asked Rya.

"The doctors do operations and experiments on people by injecting them with two computer chips one on each of their hands. Whoever is in charge is maximizing their efforts to get every man, woman and child with a chip and a symbol of the Nations United that has that 'V' shape wheat symbol. The man who escaped told me that he was shown videos of how everyone would be living in a small honey comb apartment and that money would be embedded in these chips. Paper money, gold and silver would be worthless and the people in charge would have their green tax. They would tax the crap out of us and if a group of us were to protest then they would just turn off our chips.

Nobody would be able to buy food, get a job or a car, you would be virtually powerless. When the chips turn off they would slowly release cyanide which would kill you and they wouldn't have to worry about over population because they could control it. They've actually been controlling the population by using SHAARP to control the weather and create aggressive weather patterns like hurricanes, tornadoes and earthquakes."

"We can control the weather?" asked Rya.

"We've been able to control the weather for the last fifty years," said Grant.

"How?" asked Rya

"There's a facility in Alaska that uses one-hundred and thirty-eight antennas that unleashes radio waves to the sky," continued Grant.

"I'm confused, what does the Nations United have to do with this?" asked Rya as he continued. "How does that fit in with the Ravens?"

"The Ravens are a subdivision of the Nations United."

"The people in charge have been using biological weapons on American citizens starting with the bogus Lymes Disease from Connecticut that spread all over the country, killing and permanently injuring everyone.

They've been working with companies to put additives in the food to kill people. It's known to them as a soft kill, but they had plans to do one last strike that would cause a pandemic and force everyone to take vaccines. The vaccines are worthless and cause learning disabilities, ADHD, ADD, autism and behavioral problems. It's there way of dumbing us down along with the fluoride to calm us down while our body rots."

Suddenly, there was a commotion and screaming with loud barking from the dogs and everyone walked outside. They saw it was Jerry and the militia had their guns pointed at him.

Jerry was a messenger angel that was dressed like a soldier of Rome and wore a metal armor and carried a sword in its sheath with a whip that was rolled up by his tunic. His red flaming hair was short and he had a high forehead with brown eyes. He had a stubble five o'clock shadow on his face that was reddish and high cheek bones. He was small boned with a medium build and was a few inches shorter than Sarrjel. The messenger smiled at the militia as his large white wings folded up into a cape.

"He's with us," assured Sarah as she put her hand out to gesture the militia to lower their weapons.

"At ease!" commanded Joe as he gestured for his country men to lower their guns.

Sarrjel walked up to Sarah and was followed by Rya who was curious about what was going on. Jerry looked like he didn't have good news and the angels could tell by the expression on his face. Joe watched the angels carefully and his militias as he wondered what was going on. Grant walked up behind his leader and whispered, "what's going on?" Joe gestured with his hand to be quiet.

"What news do you have?" asked Sarah.

"Master Scaven is looking for you both. I overheard him talking about you while I was hiding close."

"What does he want?" asked Sarrjel.

"He wants your lives in return for injuring Brehem. Master Scaven is one of the best warriors from Satan himself. As long as you're hidden with humans at this camp you should be safe but at some point you need to get moving."

"I understand, keep us informed," replied Sarrjel as she turned to see Rya walk towards her with a concerned expression on his face and then he stopped.

Jerry nodded as he took a few steps back and his wings spread open and moved up and down like a bird as he took to the sky. The dogs barked at the angel as it left from sight and then quieted down when they looked at Sarah who looked at them. Sarah and Sarrjel turned to look at the front of the tent, to look at Joe and Grant just before they walked back inside. The expression on their face seemed suspicious but curious as to why they were here. Sarah sighed and realized there was much work to be done to win their trust.

The militia walked back into the tent and were followed by the angels to hear what Joe had to say, " I know many of you love this area and want to stay here and fight the Ravens, but we can't stay here."

"Why?" asked Irina.

"Yeah, why not? We got the fire power," said Barry.

"They have the numbers and those creatures with the drones flying around. It's a matter of time before they find our camp and attack us," said Grant.

"What are we going to do?" asked Jason. "Where are we going to go that will give us an edge?"

"In a remote spot on a farmer's lot in the middle of the state towards Marshfield there's another militia group, about twelve militia groups, that have about two-thousand people and they have marine units that have recently joined them and want us to join as well. We would have more weapons, food and increased status."

"What if it's a trap?" asked Jason.

"This is our home," said George.

"Let's stay and fight," said Johnny.

"It's not a trap, we've been communicating Morse code for the last several hours," said Grant. "It's highly unlikely that the Raven's know about it."

"Yeah, well how would you know?" asked Jeremy.

"Because we've been doing it by radio telegraph. Almost nobody has those anymore," answered Grant.

"Tim has been in contact with them for ten years before the shit started. I know you want to stay, but we are not enough to stop the Ravens," said Joe.

"Why don't we reach out to the Militia's in Minnesota? ," asked Rya. "I'm sure they would help us."

"Then the militia chattered in agreement, "let's put it to a vote." Joe heard it but didn't acknowledge it because he believed in Marshfield.

"I'm sure they would, but we haven't heard anything and they are one-hundred and eighty degrees in the wrong direction," said Joe. "We'll postpone any decisions for today to tomorrow."

"The road to salvation is in Minnesota," said Sarah and everyone stopped from leaving to listen to her.

"We're not going into Minnesota. With the river at our back we would be trapped."

"But that's where salvation is," replied Sarah.

"What will we find there?" asked Grant. "Where would we be going if we did?"

"We would gather at the capital building and wait until it is time," said Sarah.

"Wait for what?" asked Joe slowly and annoyed.

"That is what we were told," said Sarah.

"We?" asked Jason.

"Me and Sarrjel."

"We can not and will not cross the river for something that is impossible when we have a legion of demons and the Raven army damning us to hell!" commanded Joe.

"I have told you what you must do. It is up to you to make the decision," said Sarah.

"I need to go back into town," said Rya.

"What?" said Joe.

"Why?" asked Grant.

"There's a girl I left behind and she's all I got," said Rya.

"No, forget it. We don't even know if she's still alive," replied Joe. "I risked everything to get you out, now you want to go back?"

"She is alive and is hidden in her apartment," said Sarrjel.

"We can help her," continued Sarah. "We came here to protect all of you and bring you to salvation."

Rya turned his head to look at his guardian angels, "She needs me."

Sarah nodded her head and looked at Sarrjel, "we'll go with you and protect you both."

"I don't believe this," gasped Joe as he looked at Grant, but then Sarah spoke up.

"It's the human thing to do."

"This is fool hearty," said Grant as he looked at Sarah. "We should leave this area before our enemies come."

"You people are crazy!" added Joe. "The country has gone to hell and you want to run off and risk losing your life and our position for some girl."

"Don't underestimate us as the Pharaoh underestimated Mosses when he threw his staff down. It turned into a snake and it ate the two snakes bound by Satan. They were created from the wood from the pharaoh's servants. We are stronger than the demons," commanded Sarrjel. ". . . And we will prevail."

"I'm leaving, even if it means walking," replied Rya.

"If he leaves he could give away our position to the enemy," said Grant.

"Don't worry we'll protect him," assured Sarrjel.

"We're not talking about his protection we're talking about spies that are hiding in the woods to find a way to bring down our network," said Grant.

"We'll hide, I'll creep through the woods and keep out of sight," assured Rya.

There was silence and Joe shook his head, "no, I'll have to go with you."

Grant looked at Joe surprised, "sir we need you here."

"I can't risk letting them go and alert the Raven's of our position. So I'll take them in the Jeep and we'll take a secret rout back to Hustle. How long is this going to take?" asked Joe as he turned around to Rya.

"I don't know, a few minutes to run in her motel room, pick up a few clothes and run back out," said Rya as he watched Joe nod his head to Grant.

"If I'm not back by tomorrow, you'll be in command. Take everyone to the lot like we discussed to meet with the militia down there," commanded Joe

"Understood sir," replied Grant.

Joe left the tent to go to his quarters, his personal quarters to get some extra ammunition and grenades. He walked over to the Jeep to meet with Rya and got in the vehicle. Everyone watched and hoped that he would be ok and the angels could tell that he was well respected.

Rya got in the passenger side of the Jeep and they left the camp. Sarah and Sarrjel opened their wings and flew to the sky to follow them several miles above. They drove through secret paths in the woods and pulled up from the ditch to a street leading to Hustle.

Once in town, they could see smoke in the sky, cars were turned on their side, buildings were smoldering and there was debris all over the road. Luckily there was no sign of the Ravens and Joe continued to drive as Rya gave him directions to the motel and before they knew it they were there.

"I'm going to park behind the motel. I don't want to attract any unwanted attention in the front," commanded Joe.

"That's fine, I'll only need five minutes," said Rya as he got out.

Rya watched the Jeep disappear behind the edge of the motel and turned around to knock on Sara's door, but didn't get an answer. After repeated attempts of knocking, Rya took a couple steps back and kicked the door down. Rya ran inside the room calling out her name.

"Oh thank God it's you!" gasped Sara from around the corner of the closet with a broken broomstick raised over her head, "what's going on?"

"I'll explain later, but we need to get out of here."
"Where are we going?"
"Somewhere safe."

For five minutes, Sara quickly packed everything from her closet into her suit case. Rya pulled down one of the blinds in front of the window of the room with his finger to see a black Jeep pull up in the parking spot with two more Jeeps next to it.

Inside the first Jeep, that pulled in, were officers dressed in black uniforms and in the other two Jeeps were about six soldiers wearing armor and helmets with big guns in their hands. One of the men that stepped out of the first Jeep looked like an officer with the way he was decorated. Then the door slammed shut and Rya turned his head to see it was Sarah and Sarrjel. He wondered why did they do that, but most of all how did they get by without being seen.

"What are you doing?" whispered Rya as he turned back to the window and saw the men in black uniform stare at the apartment that they were in and started walking to the room.

"I'm fixing the door you broke," commanded Sarrjel as she used her hands to repair the lock. After a sudden flash of light the door was back to the way it was.

"Our enemy is here," commanded Sarah.

"Yeah well, they heard you slam the door shut," replied Rya.

Then Sara walked out of her room and into the living room. She dropped her suitcase to see Sarah. The angels turned their head to look at the girl that looked identical to them.

"They look like me," said Sara in shock.
"It's a long story," replied Rya.
"How do we escape?" he asked as he heard the pounding at the door.

Sarah and Sarrjel looked at each other until Sara sulked, "you're suppose to be angels. Can't you do any magic."

"We don't do magic tricks," said Sarrjel. "We're not fickle."
"Only small miracles," added Sarah.

The door burst open and soldiers wearing bullet proof armor marched in with their leader. They looked around the apartment and scavenged through Sara's room.

"Sir it looks like we just missed her," said the first soldier as he showed Sara's bra and underwear.

"Are the other occupants from the other rooms, restraint in the truck?" asked the officer.

"Yes Colonel Lex," answered the second soldier.

Colonel Lex felt like someone was watching them, but he couldn't see them. He didn't realize that Sarah and Sarrjel were using their powers to make Rya and Sara invisible. They stood silent and watched the soldier tip over the couch, tables and throw clothes around the bedroom. Sara was about to gasp, but then Sarah, the angel, put her hand over Sara's mouth to keep her quiet.

The colonel stopped as though he heard her and looked around in their direction. At first Rya thought they were discovered, but then the officer snapped his fingers together and the soldiers stopped.

"Come on she's gone, we need to get back to headquarters."

There was a CB radio similar to a cop radio on the soldiers that was giving all kinds of code information from a human voice that revealed an attack from the US Army engaging the Raven Army. They left and slammed the door shut as Rya took a deep breath and crept by the window with the blinds. He watched the soldiers get back in their black Jeep.

"Well we can't go out the front," said Rya.

"Why not?" asked Sara. "If they can turn us invisible then we can make a clean escape."

"We can't abuse our power," said Sarrjel.

"Then we'll have to bust through the wall to get to Joe's Jeep," replied Sarah.

"Sarah, leave and find Joe. Tell him that we're busting through the back wall to get out," said Rya as he watched Sara freak out. "It's ok, we'll get out of here."

Sarah nodded as she carefully as fast as she could opened the front door and flew away.

"I'm scared," said Sara. "If it wasn't for you those men would have broken in my room and taken me away. I feel like a Jew in Nazi Germany," she started crying.

"No it's ok, we're going escape from this," assured Rya

"Rya," said Sarrjel from the bathroom. "There's a window here."

Rya walked into the bathroom and saw a small window that was big enough for them to fit through, "that'll work."

Joe waited in his Jeep about a block horizontally behind the motel and looked at his watch. Sarah landed on her feet in front of the Jeep with her wings wide open. Her body was glowing white and she walked quickly to Joe in the driver's side.

"The enemies broke into the apartment, but they're alright," said Sarah.

"Are they still inside?" he asked.

"No, they're on their way out from the back. Go now and pick them up!" she exclaimed.

Joe turned the key in his ignition and peeled out from Sarah's position. He drove quickly to the back of the motel and could see a woman with blonde hair fall down onto the pavement from the small window with an average sized suit case. He then saw Rya slip through it as well and when they were both out Joe twisted the steering wheel around in a sharp turn and the Jeep skidded right up to them to a grinding halt as they both climbed in the back seat.

"Go, go, go!" exclaimed Rya as he heard the tires peel and the Jeep's motor roar.

"Oh shit, we got company!" yelled Joe after he looked in his rear view mirror and Rya looked back to see the same black Jeeps closing in. "Hang on! I'm going to try to lose them!"

The Jeep accelerated faster and as they drove through the neighborhood at 70 mph Rya could see the three black Jeeps had caught up to them, but when he turned around the front he saw Sarah behind a dead oak tree on the edge of the block. The tree was huge and when she opened her wings she push the tree down with her hands and it began to buckle as they drove by and then it collapse on the black Jeep behind them. It landed on the hood of the black Jeep and because it had a large thick trunk it prevented the other two Jeeps from pursuing as well. Rya smiled and Joe laughed, but they knew they weren't out of the woods yet.

Sarah looked at the colonel and the officer in the Jeep that she totaled and with a smile she bowed her head at them before taking flight to the sky. The officers looked at each other and watched her disappear from sight.

Joe arrived at the militia camp and Sara looked around to see groups of people dressed for war. The German Shepherds were present and started barking, but once they came close to smell her they relaxed. Rya could tell she looked out of place, shaking hands with strangers that were going to be protecting them.

Grant walked up to Sara and shook her hand, "don't worry the dogs won't bite. Welcome to the Zion Militia Outpost."

"Thank you," said Sara as she shook his hand.

"Come," began Grant. "I'll take you to your tent. After Rya left, we decided to put something together for both of you."

The couple followed Grant to their tent and the second in command left them to sort things out while he went back to the meeting area. Rya and Sara stepped inside the dome tent and Sara looked around to see two sleeping bags, a back pack with his lap top inside and a suitcase of clothes that was donated to them from the militia.
Sara smiled and nodded her head as she continued to walk inside to set her suit case of clothes on the floor. She lied down on her sleeping bag and smiled as she looked at Rya.

"I wasn't going to leave you at your apartment."

"I know," she answered. "That was sweet of you."

Rya took Sara by her hand and they stepped out of the tent to the militia meeting that had just been called. Everyone was looking at Joe and his second in command to discuss the next plan of action.

The angels glided down from the sky with their wings open and landed on the ground. The dogs started barking and the militia took notice by swinging around with their weapons. The angels looked at them and lowered their hands. The militia relaxed and turned around to listen to what Joe had to say. The angels walked past the humans and stood next to Rya.

"The city of Hustle has cleared up from the creatures, but there are still Ravens combing the city for stragglers. What I want to do is get every vehicle ready to leave. I want our guns prepped and I want a team to map out a path to our new destination in Marshfield. We got a couple of drones, we should use them to spot an ambush. I would like to avoid a confrontation so we don't lose our shit and caravan. We have two days people, let's move it!" commanded Joe.

Everyone scattered once the meeting was finished Irina, Brenda and a few other girls walked up to Sara to make small talk. Rya look at his guardian angels and noticed how sad they were. After Sara finished talking to the women they move on to their daily duties of oiling guns, setting perimeter traps, watching the perimeter and cooking food.   The couples that had children were either kept in their tent or were helping prepare food.

Grant left to continue with training the less experienced militia members with weapons, martial arts and boxing. Sara looked at Rya and gestured him with her head to meet with her. He followed her back to his tent and wondered what was on her mind.

She looked at him sternly, "why didn't you tell me you had guardian angels?"

"The names are Sarah and Sarrjel I've been visited by them since I was in college."

"What are we doing here?" she asked.

"What are you talking about?"

"We don't know these people, I feel strange staying here."

"These are honest, good, people that are putting their ass on the line."

"Yeah, well the day before was a normal day and now we have crazy nut jobs in martial law outfits gathering people up like it's nineteen-forty two. Did you know I had to hide in the closet?"

"Well, how do you think I feel? I got chased down the street by a demon."

"I just hope you don't think your going to make this into some kind of editorial," said Sara

"What is that suppose to mean?" asked Rya.

"You know what I mean."

"Hey, woman I saved your ass. Two days ago I thought you were cute and sexy and asked you out. If I knew you were this shallow I wouldn't have bothered."

Then before Rya could say another word Sara kissed him. She smiled and zipped the tent up so no one could see them.

It was late afternoon. Sara walked down to the lake to bathe and clean up. Rya opened his eyes after hearing something dreadful.

He got dressed, walked outside the tent after hearing loud barking and guns being cocked. He couldn't believe his eyes when he saw the eight foot demon gliding down with his bat like wings spread apart. He had red gargoyle eyes, with dark lavender skin, he only wore a gold tunic with strips of leather that extended to his thigh and his chest was bare. He had a giant sword in its sheath on his left side.

"Everyone desist!" commanded Joe as everyone pointed their guns at the intruder and Joe walked towards the demon. "What do you want?"

"I'm Angel Hunter Malicious and I'm looking for two female angels," began the demon with a deep graveling voice. "There names are Sarah and Sarrjel. I wish to know their whereabouts and if you help me I will make sure the Ravens never come to this place."

"I'm sorry, we don't know any angels named Sarah and Sarrjel," answered Joe. "Now please, leave us in peace."

The demon let out a short growl and spread his leathery wings apart as he flew to the sky. After the demon disappeared from sight Joe took a deep breath and turned to his second in command who didn't look happy.

"How the hell did that thing find us?"exclaimed Joe

"We need to move out now. I don't trust that thing," said Grant.

"Where's Rya?" asked Joe as he looked around.

Sara washed herself with a sponge and a bar of soap. Bathing in the shallow part of the lake wasn't her style. It was cold and dirty, but she had to do something. Once she stepped out, she grabbed her towel and dried herself but then heard a noise behind her and then she turned and saw something disturbing.

Sara looked at the nine foot giant as he sneered at her with his yellow, crooked, teeth. He had a beard, was bald with earrings and tattoos on his arms and chest. He wore black clothes and leather hiking boots.

Sara was only wearing a towel over her body and had just gotten out of the lake before the giant appeared from nowhere. She backed away slowly, realizing he was here to rape her. The giant growled like a dog and touched his crotch with his right hand. He made a gesture with his mouth sounding like sex and slapped his hands together. He began laughing before he charged after her but suddenly there was a gun shot as he stopped on top of her just as she screamed with his hands on her arms. Then another shot fired and another until finally the giant collapsed. Sara's mouth dropped as she squirmed to get away from him being on top of her. She saw Rya holding a revolver directly behind the giant and lowered it as it laid dead.

Rya watched her cry and quickly put the gun in his belt as he ran to hold her. He could feel her wet hair on his chin and felt her shivering from the cold. She stammered in her crying and felt her hands on his back.

"Is he dead?" she whispered.

"I think so."

After Sara got dressed, Joe and about ten militia soldiers came to the lake and saw the giant laying on the ground. Joe looked at the huge corpse and then at Rya who nodded his head to him.

"What happened?" asked Joe.

"I prevented this monster from raping her," replied Rya.

"I didn't think those things existed," said Sara.

"We would all like to think so," began Joe. "But I think he was part of an experiment that the Ravens were putting together. Where did you get the gun?"

"I took the gun without your permission from out of your Jeep under the seat," replied Rya as he handed it back to Joe. "You can have it back."

"Keep it, you and Deputy go target practicing," continued Joe.

Deputy looked at Joe a little uneasy, " why me?"

"Because I said so," said Joe as he watched Deputy roll his eyes.

Suddenly, there were footsteps nearby and Deputy muttered something that irritated Rya, "speak of the devil."

The militia watched Sarah and Sarrjel walked through the grass towards them, that was ten meters from the woods where the camp was, to see what the commotion was all about. They were dressed the same way as before and they walked elegantly through the tall weeds. Their wings were folded back like a cape and their hair was down.

"What happened?" asked Sarah

"The young lady almost got raped by a giant," said Joe

"Giants were created by angels having sex with the human girls of Eden," said Sarrjel. "They hurt and killed many men and raped the women."

"Where were you?" demanded Joe.

"We were protecting the women and children." said Sarah.

"Why?" asked Grant. "They have guns."

"Somebody named Malicious was here," said Joe he watched Sarah turn her head from Grant to look at him and then at Sarrjel. "He's looking for you and wants revenge for something you did."

"We severely wounded his brethren, Brehem," said Sarrjel. "We expect he'll be back, but when he does we'll be ready for him."

"We can't stay here," said Joe. "We need to leave now."

"Why do you feel this?" asked Sarah. "We are here at this camp and will protect you from the Ravens and the demons that come."

"You see that's the problem that I have!" yelled Joe. "You were here, you have fore-sight to protect us and yet Sara could have been raped and killed by that giant!"

Sarah looked at the giant and then at Rya, "but nothing did happen he saved her life just as she hoped."

"You're missing the point. You were suppose to be here to protect us when that eight foot demon visited us minutes ago. How do we know you're not working for the Ravens and the demons?" said Joe.

"You would question our integrity?" asked Sarrjel.

"You would think of us as dishonest and full of lies?" asked Sarah. "That's very disturbing that you carry such distrust for your protectors and champions. You are full of ill thoughts."

"I'm sorry Sarah, but they do have a point," said Rya.

"How do we know you're with us?" asked Grant.

"We give you our word under Christ that we are not here to bring chaos," said Sarrjel.

"We will prove ourselves in time," said Sarah.

That night the angels took watch, over the militia camp. Barry, Deputy, Irina, Brenda and Jason took their positions on the perimeter. They hid up in the trees on deer stands with night vision goggles. They kept in touch by walkie-talkie and hoped the night would go by uneventful. Sarah and Sarrjel used their invisibility to hide next to the trees. Sarah felt angry and frustrated that the militia was dis-trustful towards them and even Rya questioning their service hurt her feelings.

"Are you alright?" asked Sarrjel.

"No, I'm angry that our new found friends hate us."

"Why?"

"Because if we were there when Malicious asked for us and fought him. Our militia friends would be forth coming," said Sarah

"Have faith," assured Sarrjel.

"Everything clear over here on the north side," said Jason as he stood by a fence with the German Shepherd, Bear. How about you Deputy?"

"Man, I haven't seen shit!"said Deputy as he looked down from the tree stand he was siting in with his AK-47 and looked down to see his German Shepherd Empire laying down on the leaves. "I'm up in a fucken tree freezing my ass off."

Irina started laughing, "keep it down you'll wake up the dead and the Ravens will know where you are."

"Don't be a pussy," said Jason. "It's not even forty degrees out,"

"That's too cold for a black man!"

"If you don't shut up the Ravens will know where you are," said Brenda.

"Yeah, well you put me in line with a hundred of those Raven's and I'll have a bullet in each of their brains,"continued Deputy.

"What do you guys think of the angels that are with us?" asked Irina over the walkie-talkie,

"I think they're aliens," said Barry.

"What if they're for real and they want to save us," continued Irina. "What if all they want to do is help us survive."

For a long time there was silence over the walkie-talkies and everyone was thinking. Then Jason spoke up, "only time will tell."

Rya was sound asleep in his sleeping bag and was next to Sara. Suddenly, he heard a feminine voice whisper his name and felt something shake his shoulder.

"Rya, wake up," whispered Sara.

Rya opened his eyes to see darkness and after his eyes adjusted he could see her silhouette, "what's the matter?"

"I'm really scared," she began with a chill in her voice.

"Why?"

"I'm scared we may end up in a shoot out and die. All the news on the CB radio and the visits of the demons, especially from the big one that your guardian angels weren't around to face."

"Everything is going to be fine, Sara. Don't worry about it."

"I can't help it, it frightens me. I can still feel that giant's hands over me," said Sara as she started to get emotional. "All the knowledge that I learned from college is for a future that no longer exists."

"What's wrong Sara?"

"I've been having that re-occurring nightmare that I told you about on our date. I'm walking through a beautiful forest and then it goes into a meadow. The next thing I know I'm standing on the edge of a cliff to a bottomless pit and when I look down below there is nothing there except lightning and darkness. I turn around and I see a large red demon with a black sword who charges at me to cut me in half. I scream and fall backwards into the pit."

"What happened next?" asked Rya.

"I wake up," she said.

"Sounds like an ordinary dream."

"It's not ordinary, it scares me."

"How long have you been having them?"

"For the last couple of weeks before I met you I've been having them and now that these monsters are here I'm scared, I think I'm going to die. I thought all these prophecies were fiction. I thought that if any of it did come true it wouldn't be until after I was gone in my warm bed."

"Yes but you know we would protect you," assured Rya as he heard her start crying and he reached for her hand as she gave it to him.

"Now everything that I ever wanted is gone," continued Sara as she sniffled and cried. "I'm sure I'm not the only woman who wanted a family, a good job, a nice home, with children and a dog. Why would I want to have that when there is all this violence, this hate and control from these monsters that we elected and trusted to put right that once was wrong and now these creatures are here and killing us?" Sara continued with the crack in her voice and cried harder. "All the people I knew and loved, my parents, brothers and sisters are all dead because of this evil that has risen from the darkness. Now I'm the only one left in my family and I'm never ever going to see them again," she cried and reached for Rya as he put his arms around her.

"I know, I know," repeated Rya as he heard her stop crying and she wiped her eyes while drawing closer to his face. "It's actually been on my mind since I saved you."

"What's that?" she asked.

"I'm probably the only one left from my family to and I'm sure the people in the militia have been separated from their loved ones as well. Everyone is scared Sara and I don't know what's going to happen in the next couple of days. If we hide our feelings from the people we love the most and that person dies. We become guilty that we didn't share them at all."

Sara looked at him fondly, "I love you Rya and I'll never let you go."

"No matter what happens, if the world falls apart we'll still have each other," Rya whispered and watched Sara smile at him.

"Ok," she whispered and kissed him.

The next morning Rya and Sara remained cuddled next to each other. A little boy with brown hair and green eyes squirted water in Rya's face with his squirt gun. Rya opened his eyes and watched the boy, of about five years old, run out of the tent.

"What the heck?" he replied while getting up to wipe his face with his shirt.

An Angel's Whisper

"Please stay a little longer," yawned Sara as she slowly opened her eyes.

"We need to get ready," he teased before tickling her stomach to hear her laugh and kissed her. They both got ready and Rya took her hand and they left the tent together.

Rya took a look outside to see that it was the break of dawn and that everyone was gathered outside the big tent. A lot of people were gathered including children that weren't there before. Two German shepherds stood next to Jason and was standing in front of the entry point of the tent. They suddenly walked inside the large tent.

It was early morning and the militia was dressed and geared up. Joe and Grant were inside the big tent that held all fifty members. Rya and Sara walked inside and saw Sarah and Sarrjel were already in the tent.

"Well as you know we've been visited and we need to leave right now," announced Joe.

"We should move to Marshfield and join the militia there," commanded Barry.

"Why can't we organize with the leading militias down south that are fighting The Super Highway to Canada?" asked Brenda.

"Going down to Texas is a little premature. We need to take care of our own," said Grant.

"The militias down in Texas, are fighting the pipeline, but they're losing the fight. I think we should re-assess our plans to meet with the militias in Marshfield before we try anything," said Jason.

Joe looked at Sarah and Sarrjel, "aren't you two going to try and tell me that I'm making a mistake and that we should listen to you."

"It is not our place to order you," said Sarrjel. "We have told you what you must do and we will do our job to protect the militia."

"I think we should hear them out," said Irina. "What is there, in the capital city?"

Joe looked at Irina and then at Sarrjel to hear what they had to say, " if you tell me the whole story I'll change course."

"I can tell you only what I am told," said Sarrjel.

"Who are we talking about? Who?" said Joe.

"The orders come from Archangel Michael who received his orders from Jesus," declared Sarrjel.

Joe cleared his throat and continued where he left off, "the U.S. Army had to retreat because there was simply too many of the demon creatures and the Raven army gaining ground. They have an army of those nine foot giants that are wearing kevlar body armor. I was listening in on the CB from other militias that Russian and Chinese governments have surrendered and the Ravens are using their ships to dock in California to aid in the pipe line from Texas through Minnesota, through Canada to Alaska," said Joe sadly. "The Russians and Chinese that have rebelled against this tyranny have been taking great measures to working together to stop them, but there's nothing we can do about that right now except to get moving and organize with other militias and military troops."

Then everyone started getting upset and there was a loud commotion of chatter. Rya turned to Sara as well as his two guardian angels who looked sympathetic.

"Why would those that are going along with this want to join a group of people who want to destroy lives?" cried Ellis.

"If you were promised peace by all measures and were brainwashed you probably wouldn't care who was in charge as long as you got to watch TV and eat your microwave dinner," said Joe as he looked at Deputy who smiled.

"Gullible people will believe anything," yelled Barry.

"The blind leading the blind," interrupted Sarah.

Ellis looked at Sarah and then back at Joe who continued, "I don't know why?"

"But I do know we need to stand together with another militia to expand our resources. We should go to Marshfield."

"Yes, but my family is here," said Tim. "I've lived here my whole life, I don't want to leave to go somewhere I've never been and hope everything will turn out."

Joe looked at Sarah, who said nothing but he could sense a rift forming in the group that was filled with uncertainty. There was a strong pull to rethink a new strategy and Joe didn't like making new plans over the old ones.

"Your family used to be here," replied Joe as he looked at Sarah and then back at Tim. "Your families are in a center being experimented on in a stadium or a mall and getting the chip implanted in their hand, with a number burned in their fore-head. They're also being put in re-education camps and re-programmed to take orders from their superiors. It pains me to turn my back on them, but there is nothing we can do. We can't save them because we are out numbered and out gunned and if we try to save them we'll be stopped before we break in to the first center, but now we got a new threat. That demon visited us yesterday and rest assured he'll be back with more of those things and with Raven soldiers."

Sarah then spoke up in front of everyone and the militia was quiet as they listened to what she had to say.

"My name is Sarah and I'm here to tell you that I've been ordered to keep you safe, but to ask you to come to the capital in Minnesota, we'll be safe there."

"You keep repeating yourself like a broken record, but you don't tell us anything new," said Grant.

"Do you have any brothers?" asked Deputy.

"Is there a militia waiting for us?" asked Irina curiously.

"I wasn't told, I'm just asking you to trust me and Sarrjel to guide you to safety, to take a leap of faith."

"You see it's the same old shit!" said Deputy. "Why don't you just tell us what's going on instead of jumping around like a jack rabbit on fire."

"The state capital will be full of our enemy's soldiers. Why should we go straight into a trap when we should go to Marshfield to join with a larger group of militias that would increase our chances of survival?" asked Grant.

"Archangel Michael's words are honest. He would never order me to ask fifty men and women to their deaths. I warn you that if you ignore this opportunity and go to Marshfield it will never be presented again," commanded Sarah.

"You will have protection, serenity and peace," said Sarrjel. "You will never think of home in the same way again."

"The capital is only thirty-minutes away from here and the journey to Marshfield is three hours away."

"Two hours and thirty minutes," corrected Grant.

"Right now I betcha our enemies are expecting that you are going to be taking the long road to the middle of the state and we are warning you to not take that rout. They will ambush you," said Sarrjel.

Grant and Joe looked at each other as they tried to think of what to do. The militia began to chatter in anger and Rya could tell that Sarah needed his support.

"You should listen to her," said Rya abruptly as he stood next to her. "She's my friend and she's shown nothing but honesty to me. She's helped me in more ways than I can think of."

"She's the devil!" said George. "How do we know she didn't invite that big demon to our camp? How do we know she's not bringing us to our death? There could be a trap and I've seen those aliens look nice and pretty and I've seen them look hideous. Look at her, she's a demon!"

Joe waived his hand up, "George try and get a hold of yourself."

"You look at us as demons, but look at yourselves through history from judgments you've made upon each other of different races and cultures, We are not demons or fallen angels. We are angels and we are your friends."

"If you stay you will die," said Sarah. "We know how the enemy thinks."

"Please trust us," continued Sarrjel. "We're leading you to salvation."

Sarah could tell everyone was upset and some of the women began to cry. The angels knew that it wasn't easy for them to hear what she had to say, but it needed to be heard.

"Let's give it some time. We'll put it to an anonymous vote tomorrow morning," said Joe.

"I thought you wanted to leave now," said Grant.

"No, it can wait. I wouldn't be a very good leader if I didn't let the people decide what we should do."

Grant nodded, "meeting is adjourned."

Everyone left the tent to do their daily routines. Rya took Sara's hand to leave but noticed that his guardian angels remained.

"Are you coming?" he asked.

"Yes," said Sarrjel as she gracefully walked towards him while people passed her.

Joe looked at Sarah when the last person left and she continued to look at him as though she had him all figured out. Rya and Sara were still there with Sarrjel at the edge of the tent entrance and waited to hear what Sarah was going to say.

"You have a lot of strength for one who leads, you carry many burdens and regrets. Your soul is chipped away from the pain and suffering of the people you have met. Give me your burdens and fears," said Sarah.

"I used to be a cop," replied Joe. "I don't want to lose anybody."

"I know," said Sarah. "A police officer carries a lot of burdens and is hated by the public for the wrongs of other officers."

"I served since I was twenty and have seen a huge loss of human life through homicide, car accidents and fires. I had to witness a man being burned alive and dying on the way to the hospital. So you'll understand why I'm a bit weary of trusting you. I'm responsible for these people, they need me."

"I'll stand with you," said Sarah. "You deserve a seat next to Christ at his table."

Joe slowly smiled as he looked at Sarah who looked at him adamantly. All of a sudden, there was screaming and Sarah looked at Rya who was shocked to hear machine guns go off. They ran outside to see six demons led by Malicious that were destroying the tents and campers by setting them on fire. The other demons were jumping on the women and children, clawing their faces as well as spitting on them. The saliva from a demon was acidy and similar to a viper's venom, it hurt to get spit on.

"Call your people to safety this is our arena," ordered Sarrjel as she pulled out her sword and walked towards the demons.

Joe made a run for it with Sarah and held up his M-16 as he ran outside his tent to help his country men that were running for cover and shooting at the demons. Sarah grabbed one of the demons that was on top of a child, trying to pull out its eyes and flung the creature into a tree. Rya and Sara stayed in the big tent and hid from sight. Joe and Grant drew their guns and fired at the monsters as Shadow Duke and Empire joined them.

Deputy was already ahead of the game and fired his AK-47 at the incoming demons that were the size of five or six year old children that had spiked sticks or swords. They fell to the ground with bullets in their bodies. Suddenly, Deputy was caught off guard when about twenty imps flew into his face from behind a tree and knocked him to the ground.

"Get the fuck off me you little mother fuckers!" exclaimed Deputy as he felt the imps clawing and biting his arms and face. Bear attacked the imps and managed to grab one of them by the leg before it crushed its rib cage with his jaws, but then the other imps attacked Bear by stabbing the German Shepherd with their little knives, but thunder and Thunder and Empire attacked.

Deputy wrestled them off with his gun before firing and they either fell dead or flew away. Deputy got up from the ground, but then something came up from behind him and grabbed his throat and picked him up as he dropped his gun. He looked in fear at the demon with red colored iris' and fangs similar to a vampire with lavender colored skin. He looked at the monster and could see he was muscular, like a body builder and was chocking him.

The large demon hissed at the black man, "where are the angels you fucking low life piece of shit! I can smell their flower like cunt from town."

"Eat shit bitch," said Deputy as he gasped for air. Just then Champ and Empire barked at the demon and then charged. They bit his ankles and knees, shedding blood, but retreated when the demon walloped them with his fist.

"Hey Malicious!" yelled Sarrjel to the eight foot demon who was choking Deputy. "You're a fool for coming here! You're a cockroach destined to be stepped on."

Malicious turned his head and when he saw his arch enemy he dropped the man, "Sarrjel!"

"You've seeked me out, now here I am!" exclaimed the angel as she watched Deputy scramble away to get his AK-47.

"You wounded Brehem and I've come for you!" yelled Malicious. ". . . And I'm going to rip off your wings."

"Then attack me if you can!" she declared and watched the demon pull out his large sword.

He charged at her swinging quickly. Sarrjel pulled her sword as fast as she could and caught the edge of his blade with hers. The demon's breath smelled like sulfur and sweat began to perspire from his gargoyle like face.

The militia fired their guns at the demons and imps that were terrorizing them. Deputy was on the ground and touched his throat as he took a couple of breaths to recover. Joe, Grant and Dallas fired their AR-15 Rifles at the imps that flew at them like birds with their ambition to kill them.

Brenda and Irina made a run to a camper where the single moms were hiding with the children. Brenda fired at the children like demons that had spears in their hands with her sub-machine gun.

"We have to save the children!" commanded Irina to Brenda as she fired her pistol at the demons charging after them.

Ellis, Marge and Connie fired their weapons at the demons banging on the windows and the walls. There were sixteen children huddling together like mice in the center of the trailer. The demons were laughing and mocking the women.

"Come on out of the cave you whores and give us babies!"

"We can smell your luscious bushes next to your ass!"

"Leave us alone!" screamed Ellis as she reloaded her revolver.

"You come in here and you'll be sorry!" yelled Marge as she pointed her rifle.

The demons started laughing, "we come inside to have our way with you. It is, how you say it in human terms? The joys of a man's loins is with his woman."

Then a demon popped his head in front of the window where Ellis was, "peek a boo." Then his eyes rolled back like a crazy and he yelled, "now let me the fuck in you stupid fucken bitch!"

The demons went into another trailer with teenagers, boys and girls who were armed with bats, pistols and machetes. The moment the demons opened the door they were attacked by another German Shepherd. The smaller dog ripped deep wounds in the leading demon and sent the pack in retreat, screaming.

"Thank you Lady," said one of the children as it he pet the dog on the head.

Sarah was attacked by two smaller demons almost immediately after she threw the smaller demon into a tree after hurting a child. The demons were about five foot-eight, one hundred and thirty pounds. They looked bony and malnourished as though they hadn't eaten in weeks. They charged quickly and began clawing Sarah's face. They let out a scream and tried to blind her by removing her eyes, but Sarah pushed them off. She kicked one of them as hard as she could into the woods and reached into the militia's barrel of water and turned it into Holy Water with her breath.

She cupped the water into her hand and blew it into the demon's face that was charging at her. The demon fell to the ground screaming in pain as the Holy Water burned his face like acid.

Then another demon charged at Sarah and leaped over the demon on the ground, but before it could touch her he was thrust back by lightning that ran from the angel's pointer finger. Sarah began walking towards the medium sized demon that was knocked back by the bolt of lightning and it snarled at her from the ground as it waited for its fate.

The guardian angel stopped for a moment to watch Sarrjel sword fight with Malicious and was being led into the woods. Then without warning something jumped from behind Sarah and knocked her to the ground. It was another demon with a rock in his hand and he drove it into her skull.

Jason and Barry fired their AR-15s at the imps that flew at them like large birds. They were later joined by Joe, Grant, Dallas and Deputy who helped shoot down more of the creatures. The remainder of the imps flew away from them and the bigger demons popped out from the trees with the child like demons that were the size of six year old kid and charged at the militia.

"Put down a suppressing fire!" yelled Joe as they all lined up together to mow down the invaders.

The demons screamed in pain from the bullets and some of them died instantly from the bullet to the head. Many of the other demons ran away like cowards and took to the air.

"Deputy, Dallas, Johnny and Diamond Back, go after the remainder of those things!" yelled Joe. "Barry, Jason and Tim double check our fuel supply that is hidden in one of our campers! I don't want those things getting any ideas."

"Got it," they said one after the other.

Sarrjel continued to swing her blade and as her eyes turned white, she flew to the air and raised her sword to the sky. The clouds began to move quickly and the sound of thunder crackled as lighting coursed down to strike her sword; the Sword of Righteousness.

She flew quickly with her sword and swung it as fast as she could against the demon's blade. Sparks flew from side to side against the demon's sword while the angel's sword glowed white and her wings remained open. She swung her leg up and kicked the demon in the chest, sending him through the air and taking out a small sized oak tree.

Sarah lifted her hand up and screamed as she electrocuted the demon that was on top of her and killed him. The other demon jumped on her chest quickly before she could react and clawed her already bleeding face. She screamed in pain before rising up with anger from the ground; she held the demon with her arms and walked quickly to the barrel of Holy Water and dunked him in it.

"This is what we do with vermin, beetles and maggots!" she exclaimed in anger.

The demon screamed in pain and quickly moved his legs like a child, but Sarah held him until he ceased and died. Then she pulled the demon out and threw him to the ground to watch fire burst from his corpse.

Sarah looked at the two demons that growled at her and then they flew away in retreat. Sarah's eyes pulsed with white in anger as she swung her arm up and pointed her finger at the cowards fleeing. She let out a cry that sounded like an eagle and immediately a large dust devil formed and charged after them. The white energy in her eyes dissipated to her original blue eyes.

Sarah closed her eyes; touched her bleeding head and felt the claw marks on her face. Then she reopened them and knew she had to help Sarrjel. The guardian angel turned to look at Rya sadly who was concerned for her safety and could tell he didn't know what to think.

Brenda and Irina made it to the RV where the children were and fired at the demons that were trying to break in. The leading demon that was a little bit bigger than the others was shot in the head which caused the lower creatures to scream in terror as they charged at the women and were shot dead. The smaller three foot demons that resembled children flew away and were wounded. The RV was clear and the two women walked quickly to the door as Ellis unlocked it and stepped out. Irina hugged one of the children that came out behind Ellis and there was a sigh of relief.

Sarrjel walked over to Malicious who she had knocked down and wounded. He was lying on his stomach with his face against the ground. She couldn't tell if he was playing dead or if she knocked him unconscious, but she raised her sword up to make one last blow. Abruptly, Malicious turned around while he roared and stabbed Sarrjel in the chest. Blood spilled from her mouth as she dropped her sword and fell to her knees while her clothing stained red.

"The great Sarrjel, what a pity you must die," bellowed the demon as he laughed while moving his sword in front of her. He rose to his feet and slowly moved his blade to her neck "any last words?"

Sarrjel looked at her enemy and was waiting for death, "you're the most disgusting worm that crawled from the Hole that the world has ever seen."

The demon laughed, "spoken by a true weakling of the Father."

Suddenly, a small tree trunk thrust through his chest from behind and Malicious let out a roar in pain. Sarah was behind him and her wings were raised open then the demon struck her with his arm and she fell to the ground.

Sarrjel let out a scream in anger while saliva mixed with blood dripped from her teeth as she quickly grabbed her sword and cut a deep wound into his arm, then his abdomen. There was a loud burst of howling pain from the demon as he stepped back to cover his wound.

Malicious pulled the tree trunk out from behind his back and looked at Sarrjel as he touched his wounds, "I'm going to fucken kill you cunt! I swear it! I'll slit your throat and cut you down to rip out your insides!"

Malicious lifted to the air and flew away. Sarah walked to Sarrjel and helped her up. Sarrjel was severely injured and Sarah took her arm over her head and helped her back to the camp.

"Your hurt," cried Sarah.

"It will pass," said Sarrjel as she became weaker in her steps and breathing.

When they got back to the camp the militia saw them and were speechless. There were children that were not as lucky as the children that were hidden in the RV with the mothers. They were physically scratched and burned with venom by the demons but showed their admiration when they saw the angels. Deputy, Baker, Harriet and Tim walked quickly to help Sarrjel into the medical tent.

Sarah and Sarrjel looked at everyone as they walked past to see them stare with their mouths dropped and the angel's knew that they had proven themselves worthy by risking their lives to fight the demons.

Joe turned to his subordinates, "is the gas storage secured?"

"Yes," said Barry.

"The perimeter is clear," said Dallas. "The dogs are a little bit roughed up, Bear, Thunder and Duke were stabbed but they'll be ok."

"We can't stay here," said Grant adamantly to Joe. "I know I mentioned it yesterday, but this was a well orchestrated attack. I don't think we should put it to a vote. We should get our shit and leave."

Joe looked at Grant and didn't answer. Instead he walked to the medical tent.

The angels were brought into the medical tent and the doctor and nurse looked at them to treat their wounds. Sarrjel was in critical condition and the doctor removed her white, pajama like toga to get a better look at the stab wound. The militia were creeping inside the tent to see what was going on.

"Alright everyone out, let's give them some space," ordered Joe as he waved everyone to leave and turned to look at Dr Baker and Nurse Harriet. "Can you help them?"

The doctor looked at Joe and then back at Sarrjel, "I don't know. They're very similar to humans visually minus the wings. I would say the cut is getting infected. She could die."

Joe looked at Sarah who was also looking at him. He could see the sadness in her eyes and knew that there was something wrong. Dallas walked into the tent and gestured for Joe to come with him.

"Are you feeling tired?" asked the doctor.

"Yes, but it will pass," said Sarrjel.

"You realize you do have blood in your body, right?"

"Yes, our species allows us to move in between skins," said Sarrjel.

"You've been stabbed in the chest and lost considerable amounts of blood. Can you tell me what kind of organs you have?" asked the doctor as he laid Sarrjel on the cot.

The doctor looked at the angel's naked body as he used a gauze and towel to put over the stab wounds from her chest to her back that was still bleeding.

The nurse was treating Sarah's bleeding cuts and gashes on her face with a cotton swab of hydrogen peroxide. Sarah looked like she was in a lot of pain from the stinging sensation.

"What are you people?" asked Doctor Baker. "I've read about you in Sunday School, but never imagined that I would be treating you."

"We come from another world where we have abilities and technologies that exceed your own. We can be celestial and earthbound," said Sarrjel tiredly.

The doctor turned to Sarah, "your friend here looks like she's going to die, do you have the same anatomy as humans?"

"Doctor we appreciate your care, but we're not human," began Sarah. "We will heal, I promise you, just let us rest."

The doctor and the nurse looked at each other and then Joe walked back into the tent to see how the angels were doing. He walked over to the doctor who was doing a visual physical examination over Sarrjel on the cot.

"What do you think?" he asked.

"I don't know, I've never seen creatures like these before,"said Dr Baker as he pulled the blanket over Sarrjel to cover her legs and torso.

She looked like she was fighting an infection because she displayed chills and perspiration on her face.

"Will they be ok?" asked Joe.

"I guess," began the doctor slowly. "The angel with the black hair sustained a stab wound in the chest that normally would've killed a human instantly. The blonde hair angel should make a full recovery."

Joe turned to Sarah and she looked at him, "are you ok?"

Sarah hesitated before speaking and looked at Sarrjel who turned on her side and pulled the blanket over her upper body as she shivered, "things are not so simple."

"Let them rest here in the tent," ordered Joe. "Put some extra blankets on her. If she's sick she's going to need warmth." Joe left the tent and the doctor gave Sarrjel extra blankets.

A few hours passed and the doctor was treating the militia members for injuries outside the tent and left the angels in the tent with a few injured militia to recover. Sarrjel felt stiff and rose up on the cot to stretch her back then she gasped with pain as she closed her eyes to endure the stinging, her white wings moved upward. She was naked with only her long black hair draped over her chest and the blanket covering her legs. Sarrjel laid back down and fell asleep. She felt sick and began to shiver.

The doctor walked in to check on her and watched in shock, as the wound on her back slowly began to close and heal. She was sleeping and Sarah walked over to Sarrjel to lay next to her. She touched Sarrjel's wound with her hand as she laid behind her and felt her tremble and heard her scream in pain.

That evening Rya and Sara sat together with other militia members around a campfire, roasting marshmallows and hot dogs. They were frightened about the recent attack and how it could happen so quickly. It was about six o'clock in the evening and it had been three hours since the ambush.

"They'll be ok," assured Sara as she held Rya's hand to comfort him.

"I hope so."

"I can't believe how stupid I've been," said Irina for everyone to hear.

"Why?" asked Jason.

"I didn't believe that those things were here to help us and they almost died today saving our ass."

"The one with black hair, who got stabbed in the chest, saved my life," said Deputy. "I'll never forget that, I owe her my life."

"So you think these two angels are for real when they say they want to save us?" asked Barry.

"I think everyone in the militia knows it," said Irina.

Rya and Sara didn't say anything and just looked at everyone. They had gone through a lot and didn't feel like talking about it.

"Growing up, I thought I had the whole world figured out. After the last couple of days I feel like I know nothing. The world has opened up a Pandora's Box," said Brenda.

"We've all had those fears," said Jason.

"I suppose you have always been so sure of yourself," said Barry.

"No," began Jason. "I've always had the fear that I would find myself facing death."

"Really? Tell us about it?" asked Barry as he took a swig of his beer.

Jason finished his bottle and set it next to the last ten bottles, " I've had this nightmare since I was five. In the dream I'm five years old and walking downstairs to get my dad a beer from the fridge. There is only one light and it's hard to see because the rest of the open basement is dark. I grab the beer bottle and run upstairs as fast as I can. The light goes out for no reason and before I can grab the door knob to open the door something grabs my feet and pulls me downstairs. I scream as loud as I can for my dad but he doesn't come. In the dream I see myself being dragged into the mouth of a monster."

"That's messed up," said Barry.

"The dream has re-occurred once or twice a month and it sometimes skips a couple of months, but before the rapture with the demons and the Ravens appearing I've been having this dream every night."

"I've had some messed up dreams to," said Barry.

Dallas walked over to the fire with a piece of paper in his hands. He sat down in between Barry and Jason and showed them both the piece of paper.

"Wow, what an autograph," said Jason.

"It's perfect," said Dallas. "Every part of the signature is in near accuracy of how an autograph should be signed."

Barry started laughing and then Rya spoke up, "what are you talking about?"

"I'm a professional technology specialist and I speak in hyphens," said Dallas as everyone started laughing.

"He's my man," said Deputy with a smile.

"Do you hear something?" asked Jason.

"What?" asked Deputy.

"I don't know, it sounds like singing."

"You really dig those sisters?" asked Deputy with a smile. "The blonde one is fine."

Jason gave him a dirty look as Rya started laughing, "shut up."

The scratches on Sarah's face had completely healed and she was in the woods singing. She was on the edge of the woods, near the lake where Sara met the giant and wanted to be left alone to gather her thoughts and reflect on things. Her wings spread apart and her arms were open wide as her body began glowing white. She closed her eyes as she slowly reached each high note of the soprano. She made a beautiful sound with her wings that could be described as morning rain. Sarrjel was still in the tent sleeping and gathering her strength for tomorrow. Then a little boy with light brown hair and green eyes approached Sarah from behind while she was singing. He tugged on her white dress and she stopped singing and turned around to look at him.

"Are you really an angel?" he asked.

Sarah smiled, "yes, what is your name?"

"My name is Erike and I watched you fight the monsters.

Sarah began to laugh, "yes, I really am an angel."

"Can angels fall in love with humans?" he asked.

"No, but an angel is love."

"Can angels have children? You know, little baby angels?"

Sarah began to laugh, "no, not the way humans do."

Erike began to get flustered, "well if an angel can't fall in love or have children. Then what's the point of living as an angel?"

"I am having fun," she replied. "I have fun watching humans succeed in their dreams," she continued and realized the child didn't understand. When we reach the capital you'll know what we're talking about."

Suddenly, a woman walked quickly to where Erike was, " Erike, you be the death of me." She looked at Sarah embarrassed and continued, "go back to your brothers and sisters."

The woman watched Erike run away and disappear from sight leaving them alone, "I would like to thank you for saving my son."

"Your welcome Ellis," replied Sarah with a smile as the woman looked at her suspicious.

"How do you know my name?"

"Your name is Ellis Forrest. A single mother of five, boyfriend left after the third child. Second boyfriend came in for consummation to have two more children before leaving after an argument of distrust.

Shall I go on?"

"How did you know that?" she demanded

"I know everything about everyone in this camp," answered Sarah.

"Did you mean what you said back there about bringing us to salvation at the capital?"

"Yes," answered Sarah.

"If you can promise me that my kids will have a better life in this place than this shit hole of a world then I will go with you. I owe my kids that kind of a future and I would die for them."

"I promise," said Sarah and she watched Ellis take a deep breath as though she had just taken off a huge weight off her shoulders. "You're welcome to come."

Ellis was about to turn away and stopped to look at Sarah and looked teary eyed, "what?"

"I said you can come to. This other world is a lot more forgiving than this one and you won't have to die for anyone, Jesus loves you," said Sarah with a smile but then she frowned when Ellis starting crying and ran away. Sarah felt sadness from here and realized that Ellis couldn't forgive herself.

Sarah closed her eyes and began to hymn, a little prayer for Ellis. Her wings opened up as before and her body began to glow bright from her heart chakra. The sound of morning rain grew louder and louder as she reached high notes with her singing

Sarrjel continued to lay in her cot, she was shivering and sweaty from the infection of the sword that was stabbed into her from the demon. The infection returned with a vengeance. She could hear Sarah's singing outside and felt a warmth over her body. Dr. Baker could hear her and walked over to see she wasn't looking good. He used his stethoscope to listen for her heart beat and could hear it but it was getting weaker. He looked over the wound that was trying to heal and saw it was turning red with puss coming out of it. When he touched her shoulder it felt clammy and cold. He scratched his beard trying to understand what was happening and couldn't understand why the infection was spreading. Her breath was short and every exhale there was a white breath as though she was in sub-freezing temperatures.

"I wish you would just tell me what you want me to do."

"Pray," whispered Sarrjel. "Pray for all of us and God Bless to Jesus."

Dr. Baker was shocked and looked around the tent to see he was the only one there and then looked at the angel. He kneeled down as he closed his eyes and put his hands together to pray.

Joe was in the meeting tent by himself looking at the map and modeled buildings that represented the cities and townships. He thought about the battle that had just happened and it reminded him when he lost his wife and kids. He could still remember them in his old life. Now things were different and the world would never be the same.

Grant walked into the tent, " sir I need to speak with you."

"Yes," replied Joe.

"What have you decided about tomorrow."

"I don't know, but I do know I don't want to lose anyone. We'll let the people decide."

"Sir, these people are not military personnel. They can't make that kind of a decision. You are a natural leader and militias are founded and lead on good leadership. That is why I'm making a motion for you to skip this vote and have everyone stand behind you to travel to where we need to be."

"You would have me go back on my word?" asked Joe.

"You wouldn't be going back on your word you would just be re-assessing our goals and tell them that you're looking out for their best interest," replied Grant.

"The answer is no," began Joe. "The outcasts that we have dis-trusted have just fought those demons a few hours ago. One of them may die."

"Which is why we need to leave now," said Grant. "That winged freak escaped and will come back with a big Raven army and more of those things. Look I'm sorry for the angels and I feel for them. I really do, but we can't go to Minnesota on a whim that everything will magically work out."

"I'm sticking with the vote, the people will decide what they want to do," said Joe as he suddenly heard singing. "Do you hear that?"

Grant stopped to listen and heard it, "what is that."

"Come, let's go and see what's going on," said Joe.

Rya and Sara looked into the campfire as the other militia members were talking to each other about their lives and then heard feminine singing. He looked at Sara and took her hand, "come with me."

They walked away in the direction of the singing. There was still day light and the sun was setting over the woods.

"Where are we going?" she asked.

"Can't you hear that?"

"Hear what?" she asked as they both stopped walking on the leaves.

"That sounds like singing. Jason was right," Sara continued.

Rya and Sara followed the singing to the edge of the forest to where the small lake was. It was the same area that Sara encountered the giant and Rya could feel her hand grip tighter into his.

They came to an open view where they saw something glowing about twenty feet in front of them. It looked ghostly and feminine until Rya got a clear picture of who it was.

"Sarah?" said Rya in a peculiar tone as he saw her look at him and smile.

As they walked closer to Sarah they felt hypnotized by the melody of her voice. They saw small animals walk up to her such as rabbits and ground hogs. She continued to hymn and hum and open her mouth to the sky with her arms reaching out.

Jason, Brenda, Irina, Deputy, Dallas and Barry sat around the fire, roasting marshmallows. They were talking about tomorrow and wondering how the vote was going to go.

"So if people vote to leave for Marshfield, will you go?" asked Jason to everyone.

"I will go where ever Joe tells me to go," said Barry. "If we need to go to Marshfield, I'm there for him. If he tells us we are needed in the Arctic, I'm there."

"The Arctic?" said Deputy. That shit's even colder than this shit in Wisconsin!"

"Well, what about Minnesota?" said Brenda. "It's not much better."

"oohhh," said Deputy as he shivered his shoulders jokingly. "It's too cold up here for a black man."

"Do you guys hear something?" asked Brenda and everyone stopped to listen.

"I hear something," said Deputy as he lit a fart.

"Not funny," said Irina as she got up and waved a towel in front of her.

"You heard beer and beans coming out of my ass," laughed Deputy. "That should warm up Wisconsin for the night."

Suddenly, someone walked by and the group noticed it was George, "you guys hear singing?"

"Where were you when the attack happened?" asked Jason as he ignored the question.

"None of your business," stammered George.

"You're the one that called our new friends demons," said Irina.

"You know what, I think you were hiding behind the single moms who were shooting at the pieces of shit demons," said Barry.

"Well think what you want, but I'm going to find out where that singing is coming from," said George and he left.

Then Jason heard it again, "I hear it again. I'm going to find out what it is."

Jason left with the others and passed Ellis' tent who was with four other single moms who were feeding their kids and oiling their guns. Ellis thought about what Sarah had said and it was driving her crazy. Marge and Connie looked at her concerned.

"What's her problem," asked Connie.

"I don't know," she's been acting strange," said Marge.

"Ellis, what's the matter with you?" said Connie.

"Nothing is the matter with me, I'm just sick of the world we live in and I want my kids to live a good life."

"Well don't we all," said Connie. "If the men would only do their part and stick around then maybe the world would be a better place."

Ellis stopped oiling her gun when she suddenly heard singing through her tent. She became emotional and started crying because she felt like everything was against her.

"Honey tell us what's on your mind," said Beatrice.

"I talked to one of the angels named Sarah and she knew everything about me. It was like we clicked," said Ellis.

"Well what's wrong with that?" asked Beatrice.

"I haven't felt special since I met my first love in high school. Then when he left me I felt so small and so apart from any man. When I met my second boyfriend he knocked me up twice and promised me to be responsible and we would get married and I believed him. Then he lost his job and we got into this big fight. He left me with nothing and all I have in my life are my kids. If what these angels talk about is true and there is this other place that I can go, that we can go, to raise our kids in a good light then I want to take it."

"So what's the problem?" asked Marge.

"I never went to church. My mom was a single mom and her mom was a single mom. I'm afraid I'll get shamed and shunned, but then that angel said something that that sent me in tears."

"What did she say?" asked Connie.

"She said that I'm welcome to be there and that Jesus loves me!" cried Ellis.

"I can hear singing," said Marge.

"Let's take the kids with us to see who it is," said Connie.

"I know who it is," said Ellis. "It's that guardian angel, Sarah."

"I think we should go down and watch her sing, it will be fun," said Marge.

Then Ellis nodded, "ok, let's do it. Get the kids together."

The single moms got together with their kids and followed the singing. They met with the militia members and followed each other down to the edge of the forest.

When they got down there they saw a great spectacle of lights and animals flocking around Sarah as she continued to sing. Joe and Grant looked at each other shocked and could see the entire militia was there. It was beyond belief.

The next morning Sarrjel opened her eyes and rose up from the cot. She removed the blanket and walked over to her white angel dress. She slipped it on and felt renewed as an electric current moved through her body and her wings opened up. Sarrjel had healed from her wound and was ready to resume her duties.

The doctor had stepped in with the other guardian angel, Rya and Sara. He smiled and walked to examine Sarrjel, "how are you feeling?"

"Better, thank you," she replied as she looked at Sarah and then Rya.

"Let me be sure," said Dr. Baker as he pulled out his stethoscope. "Can you open up your gown so I can take a look at your wound?"

Sarrjel looked at Sarah to get a nod and unbuttoned the back area of her angelic fabric that was still stained with blood just like the front. The doctor put the end of the stethoscope to her chest, listened to her heartbeat and then looked at the area a few inches below her breasts to see skin. It was as though the wound never existed.

The doctor looked at Sarrjel in shock, "how is this possible."

Sarrjel smiled and buttoned her angelic gown back up again, "I told you there was nothing to worry about."

"But last night I came into the tent and saw you sweating and having shortness of breath. You looked like you were going to die."

"That you did and Sarah was praying out in the woods and used the militia's energy to help me heal from the infection, as did you."

"But there has to be a scientific and logical reason as to how you healed from a stab wound in the chest, I demand to know."

"An angel's body is different than a human's. Where we come from we have an anomaly in our body that regulates the body similar to your heart."

"So you have an organ that does this?"

"Yes," replied Sarrjel. "It would be an important organ similar to your thyroid, heart and liver."

"I want to learn more," said Dr. Baker.

Sarrjel smiled and nodded, "later."

"Has the militia decided to continue with their plan with Marshfield?" asked Sarrjel.

"We're preparing to vote on whether we want to go to Marshfield or to the capital in Minnesota," said Rya.

"How do you think the vote will go?"asked Sarrjel.

"I don't know," answered Rya.

Then Sarrjel looked at Sarah, "how do you think it will go?"

Sarah shook her head, "I think the humans here will make up their own minds of where they want to go. I have no idea as to what decision this will take us."

Sarrjel looked at Rya, "if they decide to go to Marshfield then we must leave to go to the capital."

"Just the three of us," said Rya.

"Now wait a minute I'm coming to," said Sara.

"As you wish," said Sarrjel.

"But what if Joe doesn't let them leave with us?" asked Sarah.

"We must do what we need to do in order to get to the capital. We only have a small window before it closes for good and we will be stuck here forever," said Sarrjel.

"I want to come to," said Dr. Baker and Sarrjel looked at him. "You might need a doctor."

"Your kind might need you. What do you think Joe is going to think if he has no doctor to help his men?"

"I'll take that chance, besides Harriet will stay behind to take care of them."

Sarrjel nodded her head, "very well."

Suddenly, Jason stepped into the tent, "you have a visitor."

The angels walked outside the medical tent with the doctor, Rya and Sara behind them. It was Jerry and he had something in his hands covered in a gold cloth that was long and thin.

"Jerry, what news do you bring?" asked Sarrjel with a smile.

"It's good to see you to, Sarrjel. You are alive and well."

"Of course, what is that suppose to mean?" she asked.

"Nothing, it's just that you have survived the fight with Malicious."

"Well it wasn't just me but both of us," said Sarrjel.

Sarah stepped forward, "I got lucky while he had his back turned."

"I have come to give Sarah a gift," said Jerry as he gestured for Sarah to come forward.

Sarrjel stepped aside and let Sarah pass to meet with him. The messenger angel smiled and handed it to the guardian angel. Sarah unraveled it to see it was a long sword, a king's sword as it was described. It was the same size as Sarrjel's sword and as she looked at the golden handle she put her hand on it. She pulled the sword from its sheath and raised it up to the sky to see. It had diamonds on the top of the handle that were the size of a small pearl. There was fancy engravings that looked like fire and Sarah looked at Jerry with a smile but then kept her composure.

"I don't understand," she said.

"You saved Sarrjel's life and Archangel Michael commanded the smithy to forge this sword for you."

"But how did you know?" she asked.

"Because I was there," said Jerry. "And I told Michael what you had done."

"Wait a minute, you watched and knew we were in trouble, but did nothing?" asked Sarrjel.

"I'm a messenger, not a fighter. I left as soon as I learned the demons were dealt with."

"Now wait a minute, how did you get to go back to where you came from so quickly?" asked Dr. Baker.

Jerry looked at the man, "we all have are missions and I don't have to explain myself to you."

"Where will you go now?" asked Sarah.

"I have to go back. Archangel Michael needs me to return at once."

"Very well, have a safe journey," said Sarah.

Jerry nodded and smiled to everyone, "good luck to you all."

The messenger walked away and as he took to the air he spread his wings and they watched him disappear in the distance.

"Why doesn't he stay to fight?" asked Jason.

"Because he's a messenger. Messengers don't fight," replied Sarrjel.

Sarah looked at her new sword and felt glorified, "it feels so good to handle."

"What will you call it?" asked Sarrjel.

"I will call it the Light in the Darkness," said Sarah with a smile.

"We should probably get in the tent to cast our vote," said Rya.

"You go ahead," said Sarah "We'll wait here."

Jason led everyone, except the angels, into the tent where Joe and Grant had formed a line for everyone to follow. Sara held Rya's hand and looked at him scared.

"What's the matter?" Rya whispered.

"I like these people and don't want them to leave us," she whispered back.

Rya shrugged, "we can't make these people do what they don't want to do."

Grant handed each person a small piece of paper, "write either Wisconsin or Minnesota."

Each person filled out the piece of paper and folded it up to put in the army helmet. The line moved smoothly and Rya looked ahead to see Joe was waiting for the helmet to fill up. The look in his eyes was anxious and Rya could tell he wasn't sure of himself.

"Can I write down Hawaii or the Caribbean?" said Deputy and heard Irina, Jason, Barry and a few other militias start laughing.

Grant shook his head and smiled, "stop being a smart ass and make a vote."

Deputy started laughing,"I just thought I would ask. This is cool though, we'll just move from one cold spot to another cold ass spot."

Deputy folded up the piece of paper and put it in the helmet before walking through. The line began to shrink down and everyone was outside waiting for the result.

Once it was over, the tent was empty and Grant looked at Joe who had his helmet full of paper, "well let's see where we're at."

The militia waited for a long time and it seemed like it was taking all day to get an answer from Joe and Grant. Sarah had sat down by a tree as suddenly a robin flew down and landed on her leg. It chirped and fluttered it's wings as it hopped closer to her. Rya, Sara and Sarrjel watched just as Sarah whispered something to the bird and it flew away.

"What did you say to the bird?" asked Sara.

"I asked the bird to cover our perimeter as well as the paths to both locations and come back to report."

Sara looked at the angel disturbed, "you can make people invisible but you can't use your special powers to check on the locations yourself?"

"I do not wish to," said Sarah. "If I flew to check on the locations myself I would give away my position immediately. Demons and humans don't think about a small bird flying by."

Sara sighed and looked away a little discontent about her answer.

"Oh wow, that is a sweet ass sword!" yelled Deputy and he walked over to start a conversation with the angels.

"It was given to me," smiled Sarah.

"Why didn't they give you bad ass gun?"

"We use swords to shoot our power," said Sarah. "It's a lot more powerful than what you humans use for guns."

"So if you got a box of dice to use as a weapon, you can make it more powerful than my AK-47?" asked Deputy.

"Excuse me, who are you again?" asked Sarrjel

"My name is Jimmy Black, but I changed it to Xavier Blade because it's cool and I want to be cool, but people say I like to be the boss and don't know when to shut up so I'm called Deputy."

"I thought it was you, but it sounds like you have a multiple personality issues," said Sarrjel.

"Yeah, maybe I do, but then maybe I don't," said Deputy.

Then Ellis walked over to the angels who were sitting with Rya, Sara, Jason and Deputy, "I just wanted to say thank you for what you said last night."

Sarah looked at Ellis and smiled at her, "it's ok."

"No it isn't," began Ellis emotionally. "It's been so long since I've had hope. Even after my boyfriend left after he lost his job to when the rapture occurred. I've been barely able to hold on."

"I understand and I'm happy that you have come out of the darkness. Jesus will be happy to see you again."

Ellis started to get teary eyed, "can you tell me what the result will be with the voting?"

"I can't tell you because I don't know," replied Sarah sadly. "I'm sorry."

Ellis lowered her head down and wiped her eyes, "I understand."

"You are welcome to stay with us, you don't have to walk away back where you came from," said Sarah.

"Thank you," said Ellis and Sarah moved over to let her sit next to her.

"Sarah, when Joe rescued me back in Hustle why didn't you and Sarrjel follow right away?" asked Rya.

"We had to make sure that you weren't going to be pursued by the demons and the Raven's. So we remained to keep them focused on us."

"It's the same answer when we rescued your friend," said Sarrjel. "We stayed by the motel building to keep them from chasing you."

"But then how did the demons find this place eventually?" asked Jason.

"I don't know," said Sarrjel. "You guys have drones to scout an area out, maybe the Ravens have the same technologies. You aren't invulnerable to an attack, your enemies may have greater technologies to find you that we haven't been able to figure out."

"Yes, but your technologies are greater right?" asked Jason.

"Our technologies are different where we come from," said Sarrjel.

"Can you tell us where you come from?" asked Ellis.

Sarah looked at Sarrjel adamantly as Sarrjel cleared her throat and prepared to explain, "The place we come from is a civilized world. There is no crime, no hunger and everyone is rich. Everyone is welcomed into God's Kingdom."

"What about our loved ones that have passed away?" asked Ellis.

"You humans look at death in a negative way, but life only changes from one form of existence to another. When a loved one dies their soul leaves the body and goes on to the next level of consciousnesses. Most of the spirits are choosing to remain here, some of them become lost and get stuck in this plain of existence."

"Well what about where you come from?" asked Jason. "Don't they find their way to this heaven of yours?"

"Heaven is vast and infinite. I come from only a small spectrum of it and if someone isn't looking for it then they won't find it. The souls that do make it are in what you would call limbo. If the soul lived a harsh life or died in a horrific way, then they are damaged. If they go into the light and make it. They are brought to a rehabilitation to recover or what you would call a hospital," said Sarah.

"So, like, a nuthouse?" asked Deputy and then everyone laughed.

"No, not a nuthouse, more of a safe house with loving hearts," said Sarah. "Souls and angels that help wounded souls who have lost their way are there."

"This Heaven, Will we find it?" asked Ellis.

"That depends on you. Whether you're alive or in death, the Kingdom of God waits for you, but you can also bring it into your lives. Jesus himself laid down the rules for you to know where to find it, all you have to do is open your eyes and look," said Sarrjel.

"Sounds like a bunch of fables and fairy tales," said Deputy.

"Believe what you want," said Sarah.

"Yeah, well there is one thing that I believe in and that is my gun."

"Is Deputy allowed in this world of yours?" asked Ellis.

"Of course," said Sarah.

"As long as I get to keep my gun," he replied.

"Everybody has a gun," laughed Sarah.

"So wait a minute," began Jason. "I thought that if you broke God's rules you weren't allowed to be in Heaven and would be cast out to live in Hell after being judged."

"Yes the rules do apply, but they're easy to follow."

"Uh, no they're not," said Deputy. "Have you read the bible? It's like masturbating while you clap your hands."

"Our rules and teachings from the other side are not the same as the teachings in this world," said Sarrjel.

"What do you mean?"

"Those set of teachings were written about three hundred years after Jesus died and were corrupted by lesser men to control people. Whatever Joe and Grant decide if you find your way to the other side you will be told the truth and it may take several years before you remember it all."

Suddenly, Joe and Grant stepped out of the tent and all the militia members stood up including the angels, "I've counted all the votes and we're going to the capital of Minnesota as the angels have advised us."

"What were the numbers?" asked George.

"Thirty-eight to twelve," said Joe.

"Well couldn't we split apart into groups?" asked George.

Grant looked at Joe who looked like he wasn't particularly fond of the idea, "no we're not splitting apart. We decided this as a group and we'll go together."

Rya looked at Sarrjel with a smile and was happy that they wouldn't have to leave the militia.

"Now, before we get started there's going to be a lot of preparation involved. Jason and Barry I want you to get the mini drones ready. In order to get to Freeway 49 we need to make sure there is no surprises in the town of Hustle."

"Yes, sir," said Jason and he left immediately.

Everyone began to get a move on to get weapons loaded and put out the campfires. The women put away all the cooking wear in their trucks, campers and pulled out their machine guns. The men re-armed themselves with secondary weapons like handguns, pistols and long knives. Some of the men wore army vests with lots of pockets that had extra attire as well as grenades. They met together outside by the Jeeps and RVs loaded with supplies and the tents were folded up.

Joe walked up the line up of about fifty people with his clip board and looked at everyone as he passed by. Everyone was in camouflage clothes wearing helmets, but they weren't wearing the scarves over their mouths and nose to hide their identity. Joe hadn't shaved his face yet and his face was even more bristly. On the right arm of each militia, that wore a jacket, had a signa which was the United State's flag on their left arm.

"Ok I want all the children together in the middle RV so they'll get the maximum protection in case we get attacked. Jason and Barry are going to send in two drones to check for our enemies. Grant is going to lead a small team to investigate the town and make sure that we won't get ambushed," Joe announced to everyone.

Sarrjel turned to look at Sarah and Rya and walked up to Joe, "commander I want to go on the mission with Grant."

"Well you'll have to talk to him," said Joe.

Sarrjel walked over to Grant who was adjusting some large metal bracelets that extended from his wrists to his forearm just before his elbow, "sir I want to go with you on your mission."

Grant moved his right hand into a fist that held a metal lever which activated two prong like blades that extended seven inches, "why?"

"Because I can help."

Grant looked at the angel, "I thought your job was to babysit."

"My job is to ensure the survival of your people and Rya," said Sarrjel.

Grant relaxed his hand and the blades retracted back and he put on mesh gloves used for operating a cutting machine on both of his hands and put black leather gloves over them, "alright you can come, but I'm in charge."

"Yes sir," said Sarrjel.

"Understood?" asked Grant.

"Yes sir," said Sarrjel as she watched Grant put on an army jacket over his kevlar vest.

"Deputy, Irina and Johnny. You are coming with me to scope out the town," ordered Grant.

"I'm coming to," said Brenda.

"Fine you pair up with Deputy. Johnny Wylde and Irina are a team while me and Sarrjel will be a team.

The team made sure their MBITR communication worked. The radio worked the same way as a walkie-talkie but it was connected to a control panel in the master control room that was built in an RV. Barry and Jason had MBITR attached to their ears as they took off the plastic containers to look over the drones. The drones were common devices that had a camera and a light with four propellers. They weren't as advanced as the newest military drones, but they did the job well.

Grant, Irina, Brenda, Johnny, Deputy and Sarrjel loaded up in the Jeep with the two drones. Joe walked out to the Jeep to talk to his second in command.

"We'll be driving one hundred meters behind you. Use the drones before you move into the town. If there is a sign of an ambush we need to know right away."

"Sir, if this is a trap the RVs will be a sitting duck. You won't be able to turn them around."

"I know," replied Joe as he looked at the Jeep. "Take care of my Jeep for me."

Grant smiled, "permission to leave sir?"

"Permission granted," Joe replied as he lightly hit the hood of his Jeep.

Grant waved his hand and circled as the Jeep pulled out to let the other vehicles know that they were preparing to pull out. Grant pushed on the gas pedal to make it through the trail that led deep into the woods until they reached the pavement of the street. They accelerated about fifty feet and waited for the first RV to pull out into the street .

Joe was in the first RV which was more of command center than a living quarters. The driver careful drove on the narrow path, hitting tree branches on the roof that swung back in place after the RV drove by. Other campers and trucks followed suite and before they knew they were on the street following Grant in the Jeep. Instead of going down the ditch there was a man made wooden bridge that was covered by brush and tree branches. Dallas and Diamond Back cleared it off and, with help, they moved it to cross the ditch.

For miles the Jeep continued to roam down the street at about sixty miles an hour. They kept their spacing at about two hundred meters ahead of the caravan.

Grant popped a cigarette in his mouth and then exhaled, "so do you really carry a sword into battle?"

Sarrjel looked at Grant, "I carry my sword because it's my weapon and my skill level allows me to use it in many ways than one."

Then Grant shifted to a lower gear when he got to another street to turn when the radio went off in his ear, "testing one, two, three."

It was Joe, "yes, I can hear you."

"Slow down to keep our spacing at one hundred meters. We're driving big ass houses not race cars," said Joe.

"Understood."

Grant sighed and pulled over to the side of the road as he downshifted to the stretch of road and turned off the Jeep. He turned around to look at his team and saw Brenda and Irina in the back seat while Deputy and Johnny Wylde were on the rear.

"How is everyone doing?" asked Grant.

Everyone nodded, but Grant could tell the women were scared. He then looked at Sarrjel, who looked displeased.

"What's the matter?"

"You dis-obeyed your leaders orders; he ordered you to stay within one hundred meters and you kept your spacing at two hundred meters."

"Yes I did," said Grant slowly."

"You can't be trusted if you don't follow protocol."

Grant inhaled his cigarette and then exhaled, "my responsibility is for the safety of my militia behind me. If we get ambushed by creeps I need to make sure Joe and his men have plenty of time to prepare."

Grant looked in his rear view mirror to see the caravan coming and started up his Jeep. He waited a few more minutes for Joe's RV to draw closer before pulling out.

Then his radio receiver went off and it was Joe's voice, "ok proceed with the plan ."

They continued driving on the country roads until they reached Freeway 46 where they saw some disturbing things. There were cars, trucks and police cars that looked like they were bombed, tipped over or simply left on the road. Thankfully there weren't a lot of vehicles and many of them were spaced about fifteen to twenty feet apart. There were still smoke smoldering in some of the cars from the oil burning. They came across dead bodies that were on the road, some of them small children. Irina started crying when she saw the crows picking the meat from their bones. Some of the bodies were burnt as if someone used a flame thrower. Grant turned off to an exit, to take another country road so that they could avoid being seen by their enemy.

When they reached the edge of the township of Hustle from the north, they slowed down to an old Tom Thumb as the caravan drew close and then stopped. Grant turned off the Jeep and got out with his rifle and signaled his team to take their positions.

"Deputy, secure the inside of the gas station," whispered Grant.

Deputy nodded and walked to the door, Brenda covered him. Sarrjel got out of the Jeep and looked around and noticed there were no sounds of birds anywhere.

"We're in position and executing the drones to scope out the street for enemy strongholds," said Joe.

"Understood," said Grant. "We're securing the perimeter of this structure."

Grant watched the two drones lift up with their four tiny propellers and moved quickly to their destination. Sarrjel turned to look at Grant and walked over to the edge of the building.

"Hey, don't wander away," ordered Grant and Sarrjel stopped and looked at him.

The two drones split up, one went down the street that led further into town while the other one flew to the east towards the residential streets.

"Drone A is a go," said Jason as he navigated the drone with his control console.

"Drone B is a go as well," said Barry as he navigated his drone to the neighborhood.

Joe watched the colored images of the monitors that showed what the drones were seeing, "easy as she goes. The first sign of trouble I want those drones back. We only have two drones so we don't want to lose them."

"Understood sir," said Jason as he concentrated on navigating his drone.

Joe turned to his militia solider, Dallas, Daryl and Tim, "are the dogs ready?"

"Yes sir," said Tim.

"Grant, we're sending you Bear and Champ to you as you make your way through the streets to secure our rout through the township," said Joe on the radio.

"Sir, the east side of the building is secure," said Johnny on the radio.

"Deputy, is the inside of the building secure?" asked Grant over the radio.

"Yeah," began Deputy as he walked around to see merchandise on the floor. "Place is a shithole mess."

"Can you check to see if the gas pumps are on," commanded Grant.

Deputy, walked behind the register for any signs that may indicate the gas pumps were off, "I think so." The touch screen computer were still on from two days ago and he hit tender. The bell rang and the cash drawer opened to show that there was still money inside. "Sir the pumps should be on."

"Thank you," said Grant over the radio.

"Sir, I'm on the edge of the property of the perimeter on the east side, behind the building. There is residential streets back here, permission to see if there are any survivors?" asked Johnny.

"Denied, report back here at once, let the drones investigate the residential areas," said Grant over the radio. "Sir, the gas pumps are working. If any vehicles need fuel, now is the time to fill up," said Grant to Joe over the radio.

"Copy," replied Joe. "Once the building is secure, split up into three teams and take flanks of about fifty feet apart. The radio range is two-hundred meters, but I want to scout the area out before the caravan drives through."

"Understood," replied Grant.

"Do you want Champ and Bear to be sent to you?" asked Joe.

"Yes, but also send Shadow," replied Grant.

Deputy and Brenda walked out of the convenience store and walked to the Jeep. Johnny stepped out from the corner of the building and walked towards the Jeep as well. As everyone drew in, Grant had a disturbing feeling they were being watched and waved Sarrjel down with his gun so everyone could hear what the plan was.

Grant looked at everyone, "everyone's here? Our orders are to secure a path through Second street to the bridge of Freeway 49."

"Does our orders include taking out any Ravens or demons that we come across?" asked Johnny.

"Yes, but keep in mind our bullets won't kill them unless we aim for the heart or the face. They're extremely fast and strong."

"You should play your guitar like a rock star you might entertain them and they'll throw money at you," said Deputy with a laugh.

"Fuck you, I'll shove my flame thrower up your ass!" said Johnny.

"Enough," said Grant. "I know we all don't like each other, but we have our orders. Johnny, you and Irina will take flanks on third street when we get into the central part of Hustle, we're located in the northern part. Deputy you and Brenda take first street. We'll keep in radio contact with each other every step of the way. Joe is sending three of the dogs from his RV and they'll be working with us as well and we'll have two of the drones that will be moving ahead of us. I suggest we get started."

Joe turned to Tim and Dallas, "get the dogs ready."

After a few minutes when Joe felt that Barry and Jason had everything under control with the drones he got up and stepped outside where Dallas had the three dogs on a leash. Dallas was a big man that was six foot-six with a large bone frame. He was able to hold his own with the big police dogs. Joe turned to Tim who had a console box that was the size of a large tool box with rods and buttons on it.

"Turn it on," said Joe.

Tim turned it on and it made a high pitch hum sound through it's speakers. The dogs listened to it and after a few minutes they relaxed as they licked their lips.

"Interpret for me," said Joe as he looked at Tim.

"Go into town to protect Grant, Irina, Brenda, Johnny and Deputy. They are your friends. Protect them to the death against any adversary. You take your orders from them and them alone, protect."

Tim repeated what Joe said in German. Hypnosis in German was stronger than English because it was through the roots of the German Shepherd's ancestors to take orders from their masters. After the hypnosis, the frequency box was turned off and Joe nodded to Dallas to take off the leash. After the leash was removed from all three dogs they took off with Shadow in the lead to join the squad.

The squad marched on Second Street in stealth mode. They took a stance behind trees and parked cars with their guns aimed and ready at anything that was out of the ordinary, but there was nothing.

"I don't think the humans you are thinking about are going to show themselves for you to see," said Sarrjel.

Grant looked at Sarrjel with a cigarette in his mouth and gave her a disturbed look, "are you questioning my intelligence?"

"No sir," she replied. "Let me go ahead. I can only be killed by the sword of a powerful demon. Let me and The Sword of Righteousness light the way."

"Ok, bullet proof vest, knock yourself out."

Sarrjel walked ahead of the squad and had her hand on the handle of her sword. She listened for anything peculiar that might challenge her and threaten the mission. She closed her eyes and bent her head to her left and right and used her angel hearing for any signs of the Raven's or demons.

Grant raised his hands to gesture to his squad to hold off. The other militia members that were splitting up, held off, as Sarrjel continued to walk down the street cocking her head back and forth.

The guardian angel walked for eight-hundred meters and could hear things in the houses that made her fearful. She could hear panting and whispering among demons and their imps but she couldn't make out what they were saying. She could also hear chains being moved, leather wings fluttering and the propellers of the drone that was a mile ahead of her. Sarrjel opened her eyes and opened her wings as she crossed her arms while white light burst from her body. She disappeared out of thin air and Grant saw she was gone and then shook his head, thinking she had abandoned them. Suddenly, she reappeared right next to Grant and startled him.

"Stay out of the houses," whispered Sarrjel. "We have uninvited guests and hell hounds may be on the property."

"Well we can't avoid demon dogs if they can smell us," said Grant as he waved for Deputy and Brenda to continue on.

Sarrjel expressed a look of disapproval as she continued her protest, "we're making a mistake splitting up a fifty feet apart."

"You let me worry about it. Is that ok with you missy? We're big boys and girls with guns," ordered Grant as he gestured Johnny and Irina to continue on as well.

Suddenly, three German Shepherds joined them and Grant turned and smiled, "good boys,"

Grant looked at Sarrjel as he pet Shadow on his neck and ear, "let's move"

"I must go into my orb form," said Sarrjel. "It will help me move quickly through the air."

"Ok, fine," said Grant.

Sarrjel began to change shape and was almost invisible. She moved quickly to get ahead of the militia on the road and the German Shepherds panted and waited for their orders.

"Protect," said Grant as he got up from kneeling down to them and heard them growl.

Drone B moved down the street and came across no visible activity. It was like a ghost town and there were no dogs or cats present.

"Pan the camera to the left," commanded Joe as he heard the door open up and Rya and his girlfriend walked inside.

Joe ignored them and focused his attention to the camera, "distance from the squad?"

"Two-hundred meters," said Barry.

"Alright, steady as she goes, move second camera to the right so that we can see the right side of the street," commanded Joe.

"Sir, if we do that we'll be blinded as to what is in front of us," replied Barry.

"Alright, delay that order. Bring us about"

The drone stopped and turned to the right side of the street and saw something in the window of a house looking at them and then it pulled away to disappear in the darkness.

" I caught something on the camera sir," said Barry.

"Yes I know I saw that," said Joe as he hesitated to think.

"What do you want to do?"

"Joe you should pull back on the drone and have it return to the squad," said Rya.

"but it could be a survivor."

"Joe this whole thing is wrong," said Sara. "Do you think that after the Ravens broke into every house and took everyone that there would be a living person left in this town?"

"Let me make the decisions," said Joe. "It could be a survivor. Move the drone to the window so we can be sure."

"Yes sir," said Barry as he navigated the drone back to the house with the front window and the dark silhouette.

Sarah opened the door and walked in after eves dropping, "that house has a demon in it. You should regroup that device with the squad."

Joe ignored her and watched the view screen as the drone approached the window to see darkness, "steady as we go Barry."

The drone hovered up to the window to look inside and then suddenly something horrific slammed up against the window and cracked it.

Barry let out a scream, "oh shit! It's not human!"

"Bring it back, bring it back!" yelled Joe as he had watched the creature slam up against the glass.

"Take it easy," said Jason as he looked at Barry. "We're in here and that thing is about a mile away from us."

"Those things are still scary," said Barry.

Joe spoke into his radio, "attention Grant and militia squad. Do not go into the houses, that's an order."

Grant stopped where he was and raised his finger up to tell his team to wait, "what if we come across civilians?"

"There are no civilians in the houses," said Joe. "They've been taken away by the Ravens."

"Understood," said Grant. "Sir, we're about two miles from the bridge and entering the southern part of the township. You should make a move to the gas station and fuel up, it's secure."

"What is the present status of what you see?" asked Joe.

"Not good, it looks like there was a riot and pandemonium. There are still some cars that are on fire. I see bullet shells from shot guns and broken glass that I think were filled with gasoline. I think the civilians were loaded up onto a bus and taken away," replied Grant.

"Proceed and keep me informed," commanded Joe.

Rya looked at Joe as he leaned back in his chair, "they did take towns people to internment camps. They almost took me before you saved my life."

"Yes they probably did take everyone and load them on a train like cattle to a happy farm where the pastures are nice and green, but our mission isn't to rescue them. Our mission is to go to the capital," continued Joe as he looked at Sarah. "Where we'll be safe and sound, right?"

Sarah didn't say anything because she could tell he was aggravated from changing his plans to go to Marshfield. The guardian angel looked away and held the golden colored handle of her sword and hoped that they would be able to make it through town to get to their destination.

Grant reached the bridge that led to the southern part of town and could see Sarrjel move in as an orb of light that was reflected from the sun at the end of the bridge and entering into town. He held out his hand to stop the squad as Drone A moved past them and across the bridge to make sure the coast was clear before entering. Grant took a deep breath and hoped he wasn't walking into an ambush.

The three German Shepherds sat next to Grant panting and waiting for his orders. Grant turned to Johnny and Irina and nodded for them to move forward. Johnny and Irina made a move to the right side of the bridge but only moved incrementally because they would have to stoop below the brick wall that was about two and a half feet high.

Grant turned his head to Deputy and Brenda and gestured with his hand for them to move out. They moved quickly, like Johnny and Irina, and got about half way to the bridge running in a stooped position on the right side of the bridge when suddenly something caught Grant's eye. It was in the distance of about fifty meters from them and the bridge and looked like a small airplane. It measured about nine feet in length and seven feet in wing span. Grant new what it was right away and took cover behind the two and a half foot tall pillar on the right side of the bridge.

"Take cover team, we have a Predator Drone taking root," commanded Grant as he watched the craft take flight.

Johnny and Irina stood still where they were and kept themselves stooped along the bridge. Deputy and Brenda laid down on the pavement to keep from being seen. Grant could hear heavy breathing from his team mates over the radio

"Looks like it's continuing it's patrol, let it continue on," said Grant as he slowly pulled out his binoculars too see if there were any drones on the other side of the river.

"Sir, the Predator Drone has passed, can we get going?" asked Johnny.

"Not, yet. I'm scoping for any hidden military drones on the other side of the river," said Grant.

"You didn't do that shit before we got on the bridge?" asked Deputy over the radio.

Grant didn't say anything and continued to scope out the edge of the river that met with the Minnesota side.

"It's clear, let's get a move on," commanded Grant on the radio.

"Drone B is coming up on the bridge," said Joe over the intercom. He pinched the speaker with is finger as he spoke to Barry, " keep the drone below the pillars on the bridge just in case we may have someone watching us."

"Yes sir," said Barry as he navigated the drone on the main street and lowered it down a foot, just above the road.

The squad made it past the bridge and moved quickly past the railroad bridge up the hill. Grant split the German Shepherds up with each team, Bear went with Johnny and Irina while Champ went with Deputy and Brenda. Shadow stayed with Grant and when they got to the crossroads where there were new streets splitting off from the main street Grant nodded to Irina and Johnny to take third street. Deputy and Brenda walked down through a neighbor's yard to get to First Street. Deputy noticed that Champ was sounding uneasy walking through the yard and began smelling dog dong that was near the fence.

"Come on, no time to smell dog shit," whispered Deputy as they walked on a path past a window on the right side and suddenly a beast with red eyes emerged through the darkness of the window and growled at them.

Johnny and Irina walked quietly on the side walk on the next street. There was silence around them and they kept their fingers on the trigger. Bear panted as he continued ten feet ahead of them.

Johnny put his finger on the receiving end of the radio, "sir, this area is dead."

"Stay on course and keep communicating to all of us," said Grant. "We should get through the town in about twenty minutes. If all goes as planed."

"Continue to keep me informed," said Joe. "We're leaving right now to get fuel at the gas station. Once we have safe passage we'll be leaving the northern part of Hustle to get on Freeway 49."

"Copy that," said Grant as he continued to walk quietly with his M-15 Rifle. Shadow continued to walk next to him, panting and making a light whimpering noise

"Copy," said Deputy as he looked around cautiously. "We're a few miles out by the old toll bridge and there ain't nobody around, but I feel like we're being watched."

Grant stopped in his footsteps and whistled lightly for Shadow to hear and stopped, "keep your distance from the yards and don't go into the houses, that's an order."

"Copy that," said Deputy as he looked at Brenda and covered the mic. "I was hoping to snoop into an old ladies house for an apple pie."

Brenda started to chuckle lightly and looked around cautiously with her gun ready to fire, "it looks like they scooped everyone out of here. I wonder where they put them?"

"Don't know, don't care. I just want to get the hell out a here," replied Deputy. "This place gives me the creeps."

Sarrjel flew along the sidewalk a few feet in the air in the shape of an orb and then stopped. She knew that going into the houses was forbidden because there was a chance of running into a demon, but she came upon a house that tickled her fancy and flew over to it. The door was broken from forced entry and Sarrjel changed her orb shape to a ghostly white silhouette of a giant eyeball that was the size of a large kick ball with eyelashes and flew through the doorway.

The house was a mess and looked like there was a struggle. Fruits in a dish on a table had spoiled and there was darkness from along the living room. Sarrjel flew through the living room, past the couch and comfort chair where there were red glowing eyes staring out. Some of them looked angry, sad, evil and deceitful. Sarrjel flew into the kitchen to see broken dishes and the refrigerator door was open with the light on. The eye flew up to it, making a hum noise and closed it. After exploring the other room and finding nothing she decided to return the way she got out but when she did she was startled to find the whole house in pitch darkness with hundreds of red eyes staring at her with destructive glares. Sarrjel changed to her normal angel self and lit the hallway with a powerful brilliance of light.

"I walk the valley of evil and show no fear of what lies before me," said Sarrjel as she looked at the red eyes that dissipated or turned away.

"Get out of here, this is our domain now just as all the structures belong to us now," screeched the demons.

Sarrjel held her sword as she walked the dark hallway and made her way out the door of the house. She had made a mistake and realized that all the houses were haunted by demons now and could never be freed unless they were blessed by the light. Sarrjel turned around to the house and felt sad but took a breath as she changed form back to her orb and continued her quest to the edge of town where the bridge was.

The squad continued to move through the township on main street until the area became less residential and more business oriented. Grant and Shadow reached the blinking stop light and halted position. Drone A was right behind them and turned around to the rear to make sure nobody was behind them.

"Deputy, what's your position?" asked Grant over the radio.

"All clear down here," said Deputy on the radio as he waved his hand to Grant who was up on top of the hill at the stop lights. "It's dead as shit down here."

"Stand by," replied Grant as he looked at Shadow and then Drone A as it turned from behind to look at Grant. "Johnny what is your status?"

Johnny put his hand up for Irina and Bear to stop as they approached the end of the street, "it's been pretty quiet over here. Sir, is it possible there are civilians hiding in the houses that we could rescue?"

"No, by no means are you to enter any of the houses. Our orders are to seek safe passage and get the hell out of here," said Grant.

"Yes sir," replied Johnny.

"But sir what about the children?" asked Irina emotionally. "If children are alive we should try to save them."

"Our orders still stand. Do not by any means enter any of the houses. It could jeopardize our mission and give our position to the Ravens."

"Yes sir," said Irina.

Johnny and Irina walked slowly down the street on the sidewalk on the right side. There were cars that were burned, some of them were overturned. There were dead bodies on the streets, some of them had been set on fire. Irina gasped as she saw the chard bodies of children on the sidewalk.

Bear panted while walking ahead ten feet in front of them and then looked back at Johnny. Johnny looked around the neighborhood and heard nothing. There were no dogs barking from the houses, no birds chirping in the trees and no squirrels. He held his flame thrower as he looked from his left and his right.

"Irina," whispered Johnny.

Irina turned her head back at him, "what?"

"Get behind me," he ordered in a whisper.

Irina stopped where she was and let Johnny walk past her, "don't walk directly in front of me. If we get one of those things in between us, you'll be set on fire."

"I would get out of the way," said Irina. "I'm not as stupid as you think."

Johnny looked to his right to a house next door and saw something with red eyes glaring at him through the front window and then it disappeared. Suddenly, he heard a gasp and turned around to see Irina looking at something in shock. The expression on her face was happy.

"It's the children, they're alive," she whispered.

Johnny squinted three-hundred meters kiddie corner across the street from where they were and they saw a swing set and what looked like a small table with chairs. Three children were playing on the swing set.

Irina put the sling of her gun on her shoulder and started to make a run for it until Johnny stopped her by grabbing her arm, "what are you doing?"

"The children are alive!" she gasped with excitement.

"We have our orders," said Johnny.

"Yes, not to go into the houses, but the children are not in the house. They're outside," she exclaimed as she pulled her arm away.

Johnny took his hand off her and let her go. He watched the short, pony tailed woman in camouflage with the helmet walk towards the house with the children in the front yard playing. He looked at Bear who looked back at him in silence but he could tell by the look in the German Shepherd's eyes that it wasn't good.

Irina walked up to the children and smiled, "hello, where are your parents?"

There were three children; there were two boys with brown hair and green eyes. They were wearing overalls and blue t-shirts with a bowl hair cut. They were about four years old and were swinging on the swing set. The little girl was the same age as the boys. She had blonde hair and was wearing a blue dress and white stockings.

The little girl looked at Irina innocently, "mommy and daddy are gone. What is your name?"

"My name is Irina."

" My name is Katie and Toby and Chad are my friends. You're welcome to stay with me."

"You and your brothers can come with me," said Irina. "We can protect you."

"Will you stay for tea?" said the little girl as Irina walked over to her table with tea cups and a pot.

"Of course," smiled Irina as she sat down in front of her. "This is quite the table of tea. Did your mamma make this?"

The little boys got off their swing and ran over to the table to have some tea. The little girl poured the pot but there was nothing inside. Irina touched the plastic tea cup that was empty and looked at it. It was obvious they were role playing.

"Lucile is coming out with cookies," said the little girl. "Would you like a cookie? They're really good with chocolate chips."

Irina looked at the little girl with concern and suspicion, "is there anybody else in the house?"

"No, just Lucile," said Katie with a smile.

Johnny crept slowly to the house that Irina was at with Bear and was behind a large oak tree across the street. Bear started to lightly whine as he opened his mouth to yawn. He turned his head to Johnny and then looked in the direction of where the children were and began to growl lightly. Johnny saw this and had a funny feeling. He put his flame thrower in a sling on his back and pulled out one of his sub-machine gun and kept the safety on.

The boys got off their swing and ran over to the table to watch Irina and Katie play thumb war. They were laughing amongst themselves as they continued to play.

"You're pretty good,"said Katie with a giggle.

Suddenly, the front door opened and it was another little girl that was about seven years old and wore blue jeans and a white t-shirt. In her hands was a tray of cookies and she walked over to Irina and the children. Johnny looked at Bear who lightly growled again and then charged. Bear ran across the street as he heard the word protect echo in his ears. Johnny followed from behind and they stopped just before they got to the children at the table.

"You were not invited!" yelled Katie.

Johnny pointed his gun at the children and heard his dog growl and bark at them, "time to move on Irina, let's go."

"Johnny put the gun down. They're only children and their parents are gone. We have to take them with us," demanded Irina.

"No, we're not taking anybody with us. That wasn't our orders!" yelled the commando.

"Do you want a cookie? My name is Lucile."

Johnny turned around and kicked the tray of cookies from her hand. The girl started crying and screamed before running back in the house.

"What are you doing? She's a little girl!" yelled Irina as she got up from her chair.

Bear started growling loudly and bared his teeth at the children. Johnny put his hand on Bear's head to comfort him.

"We are human beings! Not monsters! These are the children and they have no parents. They need our help and I'm not going to leave them here without anybody!" cried Irina as suddenly the rest of children got up from their seats and ran into the house.

"Look at what you've done!" exclaimed Irina as she ran into the house.

"No Irina, don't go into the house!" yelled Johnny, but it was to late.

The door slammed shut behind Irina and she pulled her gun from it's sling around her shoulder. The house was dark inside and as her eyes adjusted to see light coming from the windows in the kitchen and she realized she screwed up. Window curtains were over the windows in the living room and the lights were off. Irina heard the children laughing and running upstairs and someone was in the kitchen. Irina held her gun tightly and put her finger over the trigger guard while her thumb hovered over the safety. She felt scared because she was in darkness and felt like she was being watched. As Irina walked past the furniture of the living room hundreds of red eyes were looking at her. Some of them looked weary, a few looked sad, but almost all of them looked angry.

Irina walked into the kitchen slowly as she felt her adrenaline rush and her neck began to tingle while her shoulders tightened up holding her AR-15 ready to fire and she called out, "hello?"

There was no answer, but she saw a glimpse of Katie running out of the kitchen, laughing to herself. Irina lowered her gun and ran to try and follow her but when she got the other side of the kitchen to where it met with the living room she was gone.

"Katie," said Irina but then she heard a terrifying voice in the darkness.

"There is no Katie," it said in a deep, growling voice. "You stupid bitch. You dare to come into this house."

"Who are you?" she stammered as she held her gun tightly in her arm and heard the sound of wicked laughter.

Johnny stood in front of the house and was upset. He was conflicted and was trying to figure out what to do next. He knew he had his orders and was told not to go into the houses. He also knew he was responsible for protecting Irina while they did their scouting of the neighborhood.

"I told her, not to go into the house!" exclaimed Johnny to himself as he paced back and forth. "I told that bitch not to go in the fucking house and she goes in the God damn house!"

Irina quickly ran to the door and tried to open it but it was locked and then something grabbed her and threw her back onto the coffee table and she hurt her back. Irina pointed her gun at darkness as she watched fifteen humanoids in oily demonic forms walk out from the wall and reached out for her with their hands.

"I can smell your cunt," said one of the shadows that reached its hand out and touched her face.

"What do you want from me?" said Irina in a scared tone in her voice.

"We want you," said another voice with a screechy tone.

"and we want to fuck you," said the figure with a deep voice. "Make you into our sex slave day and night while we drive nails in your limbs and cut out your tongue."

"If you come any closer I'll shoot you," said Irina as she turned off the safety from her gun.

The black figures that looked like shadow people laughed at her before backing away away into the wall and disappeared, but the red eyes in the walls still looked at her with angry expressions. Irina took a deep breath as she got back up from the floor and groaned from the pain in the middle of her back which felt like a nail was in her vertebrate. She heard noises upstairs that sounded like children playing and groaned in pain as she resumed her duties.

"The children," whispered Irina as she managed her pain and tried to move quickly upstairs.

When Irina got upstairs she was in a dark hallway. She looked around and listened for the children playing. She held her gun tightly expecting to be ambushed and followed the sound down the hallway into the room on the left. The door was a few inches open and Irina could hear the children playing just on the other side. She put the safety on, on her gun, and peered in the room from the crack of the door that had a little bit of light from a lamp.

There was Katie and the two boys who were playing with dolls. Katie had a doll and was fore-playing a woman.

"Hi my name is Irina and I like to play with children, would you like some tea?"

"No, but I would like go to the movies," said one of the boys with what looked like a GI-Joe doll. "After I take you to dinner."

Irina started to smile as she began to relax. It was so cute the way their high pitched voice sounded so sophisticated and adult like.

"No, you can't have her," said the other boy with another doll that looked like a man and he also used a toy dog that looked like a beast with red fur and red eyes. "I want her all to myself." Then the boy's voice changed to a deep masculine voice. "She is my whore and belongs with me in my chambers of pain while I take her fresh juices and fuck her up the ass." Then the little boy moved the toy dog up to girl doll, "I'm taking your head off bitch!" Then the toy dog took off the girl doll's head off as the boy made a growling and barking noise.

Irina stopped watching and felt sick to her stomach. She turned and looked around the hallway. She realized that they weren't children at all but little monsters that tricked her into the house. Irina took a deep breath and turned her attention back to the presumed children to watch them play. They continued to play with the dolls and the boy with the toy dog played with the head of the doll that was Irina. Then suddenly, Irina heard some noise in her right ear and turned her head to the wall but saw nothing then when she turned back to look in the room the children were gone and in their place were imp like demons that had large wings.

"Now you are going to die!" yelled the imp with Katie's voice and they all looked at Irina through the crack of the door.

Irina gasped in fear as she felt breathing from the wall in front of her and then growling. Irina turned her head to look face to face at a dog. Irina screamed in terror as she backed away slowly from the beast. It looked like a large German Shepherd or a wolf with long flaming red fur and glowing red eyes. Its growl made it sound more violent and aggressive than any dog she knew.

The militia soldier pointed her gun at the monster on four legs that jumped down from the wall and walked slowly as it snarled at her. It bared its teeth and barked at her. Irina turned off the safety and fired her gun at it until she ran out of bullets. The creature stumbled back from the shots to the shoulders and chest but then got angry and charged after her. The beast lunged forward, grabbed the gun with its jaws and scratched her neck and chest with it's dog like claws. Irina screamed in pain as it bit her hand with its sharp teeth. She moved her hand quickly before it could be amputated which caused deep gashes from her wrist to the middle of her hand.

She fell and crawled back along the hallway towards the stairs where she had come up. The demon dog walked towards her as it licked its lips while growling and Irina started crying.

Johnny heard the gun fire and heard Irina screaming in terror as did Bear and they both charged to the door. The militia kicked the door as hard as he could. He pointed his sub-machine gun at the door knob and blew it to pieces. Bear saw the window to the living room and heard the German words from Tim to protect. The German Shepherd growled loudly and charged at the window, busting through the glass.

Irina gasped in relief when she heard the sound of broken glass and the sound of the door busting in. Bear ran up the stairs where Irina was and attacked the hell hound. Irina watched as the two animals fought viciously.

Johnny entered the house and pulled out his other sub-machine gun. He open fired on numerous demons running and flying out of the walls to attack him. Johnny fired both of his machine guns at one creature to the next. The demons were mowed down one by one.

A demon ran up quickly behind Johnny and cut his chest with a knife. Johnny grabbed the demon's arm after dropping his gun and then turned around to kick him. Another demon tackled him down and Johnny shot the creature with his gun.

Bear and the hell hound rolled around on the floor, trying to rip each other apart. Irina froze as she heard them both growl and snarl at each other. There was blood all over the carpet and when Irina awoke from her shock she realized she had a pistol in its holster on her belt. Bear started crying when the hell hound took a bit out of his front leg. Irina pulled out her gun with her bloody hand and got up from the floor. The hell hound was severely wounded by the German Shepherd, but got the upper hand when it bit into Bear's chest after crushing his front leg. The beast opened his mouth and was about the bite into Bear's head when it heard a shot and felt something in its neck. Then multiple shots were fired and the hell hound retreated down the hallway and ran into the room where the children were. Irina took a deep breath and saw Bear laying on the floor looking at her with a gaze.

Johnny fired the last of his rounds and quickly slipped on what looked like welders goggles. He pulled out his flame thrower, turned it on and shot a ten foot stream of fire at the remainder of the demons that were still alive. He walked around the bottom floor and continued to fire his flame thrower down the hallway. He walked down the hallway and entered all the rooms. He fired his flame thrower at the demons in the room coming out of the walls to attack him. When Johnny finished what he was doing he quickly moved to the stairs and met with Irina.

"Are you alright?" he yelled.

Irina didn't say anything right away and looked at Bear lying on the floor, "yes."

Johnny looked at Bear and then back at Irina, "come on we got to go!"

Johnny holstered his flame thrower, kneeled down and grabbed hold of Bear. He picked him up and they moved quickly down the stairs and out of the house as the fire spread.

Once they made it outside and across the street on the sidewalk Johnny turned around to watch the house burn down. He turned to look at Bear who was limp and crying from his wounds. Irina was shaking and looked at Johnny as her hand continued to bleed.

"Jesus," he said as he pulled out some gauze and applied it over her right hand.

"This is all my fault," she cried. "I'm a stupid woman for going into the house."

Johnny didn't respond and held her hand tightly to stop the bleeding and heard her cry in pain, "we need to stitch this up. You're lucky I have a first aid kit with me."

Irina looked at him teary eyed and took a breath as she looked at Bear with sadness, "he saved my life. There has to be something you can do for him."

"There is nothing I can do," replied Johnny as he pulled out a needle and thread and was cleaning out the wound and was about to push the needle into Irina's hand.

Suddenly, there was a noise on the walkie talkie and Grant was on the other end of it, "Johnny what's your status? I thought I heard something in your area?"

Irina looked at Johnny before he picked it up, "all clear, no sign of activity."

Then the walkie-talkie went static and they heard Grant answer back, "copy that."

"Thank you," said Irina. "Thank you for not telling Grant."

Johnny looked at Irina, "we're not out of the woods yet."

Sarrjel continued to move through the township in her orb form. She flew past bars, gift shops and a sub sandwich restaurant. There was still no one in sight and cars were smoldering in smoke. Suddenly, she stopped at the bridge and took on her angelic human form. She couldn't believe what she saw and gasped as she shook her head back and forth. The middle of the bridge had been blown apart and there was no way to cross. Sarrjel changed back to her orb form and flew back to report to Grant.

Grant waited on the radio for Joe to answer back. The sun was overhead and sweat perspired over his forehead. Deputy and Brenda maintained their position about one-hundred and fifty feet down the street.

"Sir, our canteen is empty, permission to enter the library to use their bathroom," said Deputy.

"Can you wait a few more minutes?" asked Grant. "I'm waiting for Joe to give me orders to move forward."

"Yes sir," said Deputy. "But by that time I'll piss my pants."

Joe was at the gas station on the edge of town and they had just finished fueling up their vehicles. The militias were rolling up barrels of fuel on their trucks, campers and trailers. They needed the fuel in case they were headed in an area where the gas would be scarce.

"Come let's move it, move it, move it!" yelled Joe as he mustered the speed from each of his militia members.

"Why do we need all this fuel?" asked Rya.

"In case we have a rainy day," said Joe.

Sarah walked over to Rya and looked at Joe, "what if we can't take it with us where we're going?"

"We don't know if your secret haven is even real," began Joe with a bit of discourse in his voice. "Have you ever heard the saying; hope for the best but prepare for the worst?"

"You can't expect to carry all this fuel with us to the capital where we'll meet with salvation," said Sarah.

"How about this, you let me worry about me and my people and you lead us to this place you call home. Is that ok? Can you accept that?" asked Joe.

Sarah walked away and Rya was behind her, "Sarah it'll be ok."

Joe ignored them and went to his radio to talk to this squad, "Grant we're all set to get on our way. Is the road to the bridge clear?"

Grant responded, "So far so good, it's now or never." Suddenly, Grant turned to see Deputy waving his hands in the air and almost forgot about his request. "Sir, Deputy needs to use the bathroom to fill up his canteen and use the toilet."

"Can't he use the river?" asked Joe over the radio.

"Man, fuck that!" exclaimed Deputy over the radio. "Black men don't drink out of toilets. I need a faucet of drinking water and a toilet to take a shit!"

Joe started to smile and laugh, "Deputy go ahead but make sure you bring Brenda and Champ to cover you. I don't want you spending all day over there either."

Brenda looked at Deputy and gave him a disturbed look before looking at Champ who whined and yawned.

"She can hold my gun," said Deputy as he blocked the mic. "You can hold an AK-47 without blowing your hand off right?"

"Shut up," she replied.

Grant watched Deputy, Brenda and Champ head to the public library which was part of a police station. Suddenly, Sarrjel appeared before Grant and scared the shit out of him

"Christ, don't do that," gasped Grant as he held his gun at her and then pulled it back.

"Sir, the bridge is blown."

"What? No way," said Grant.

"It is," said Sarrjel. "If the caravan continue this way there is a risk that we'll be ambushed."

Grant took a deep breath and sighed as he spoke on his radio, "Joe we got a problem."

"What's the problem?" asked Joe as he sat in the driver's seat ready to pull out and head down main street.

"The bridge is blown, there is no way to cross," replied Grant. "What do you want to do?"

Joe closed his eyes and shook his head as he tried to think of what he was going to do next, "how bad?"

Grant looked at Sarrjel and she answered through the microphone, "at least fifty to seventy five feet."

Joe got out of the large RV camper and looked at the militia members load up in their vehicles. He saw Rya, Sara and his guardian angel get on board another truck to get moving. Fifty to seventy-five feet seemed do able to get something built to cross, but it would mean leaving their stuff behind. There had to be a way to get to the other side of the river with their equipment, thought Joe. Then he got back on the radio.

"Grant stand by, we're on our way to your position, stay put."

"Understood," replied Grant as he looked at Sarrjel.

"He's putting everyone in the caravan at risk by coming here," said Sarrjel.

"If that's what he wants to do. Everyone that voted for this journey are on their way," said Grant.

Sarrjel didn't say anything and only expressed the look of dis-content. She wanted to get to the capital but didn't want to risk lives from the broken bridge.

Deputy, Brenda and Champ walked into the library carefully, just in case there was an intruder. Deputy walked past the front desk to look for the bathroom and saw the doors. A smile emerged and he walked inside the men's bathroom, unzipped his pants and sighed in relief.

Brenda walked with Champ as she looked around to see the computers were on, papers were on the floor there was blood on the wall and a body of an old woman, laying on the floor.

Joe walked back and forth slowly, trying to figure out how they were going to get across the river and was met by Tim, Dallas and Diamond Back Daryl. They looked at their leader with concern and wondered why he was pacing back in forth with a worried look.

"What's going on?" asked Tim

Joe looked at Tim with a discouraged look, "the bridge is broke. There is a fifty foot drop in the middle."

"So we're basically screwed?"

"Pretty much," grimaced Joe with a disdained expression. "I was thinking we could use the welding tools to add an extension to the old toll bridge and get our caravan through that way."

"There's no way to cross the broken bridge at all?" asked Tim.

"No," answered Joe.

"What about emptying the caravan and crossing with the air rafts?"

"Well, we could do that," said Joe as he looked at the ground and then back at Tim. "But we just filled up on all this fuel and I wanted to use it as leverage against our enemy.

Suddenly, Joe saw Sarah and Rya walk towards him and Rya asked, "what's going on?"

"We got a problem," said Joe.

"You look worried," said Sarah.

"The bridge is broken with a fifty to seventy foot long drop. The closest bridges to cross into Minnesota are miles away and we don't have time," said Joe.

"Give me your worries and let's meet with the squad to look at the river," said Sarah.

"What kind of nursery rhyme crap is this?" asked Tim. "Give us your fears, give us your worries and have faith."

"You mock me?" asked Sarah. "If you understood as I do that you must bring the Kingdom of God into your heart and mind after you give your troubles to the Lord."

"Where is Sarrjel?" asked Rya. "How is she?"

"She's fine," said Joe. "She's waiting for us."

"Are we leaving?" asked Sarah

"Yes," said Joe feeling a little more confident that there might be a light at the end of the tunnel.

Joe turned to Tim, "let's mobilize."

Sarah looked at Joe and slowly lowered her head gesturing him to be at ease and relax, "everything will work out."

Deputy filled his canteen using the water from the bathroom sink and drank it. He opened the bathroom door a little bit with his gun pointed upward and then held it with both hands as he looked around for trouble. He knew he was foolish for not playing it safe earlier, but he had to use the bathroom for dire need. When he found nobody around except an old lady dead on the floor he began to look around for Brenda.

Brenda was in the library's break room eating food out of the refrigerator. There was a ham sandwich and a cold noodle dish with ham, onion, salami and mayonnaise. She loaded her paper plate that she found in the cupboard and started eating while sitting down to relax. Champ looked at her and licked his lips. Brenda threw him the other half of the ham sandwich and he ate it.

Joe led the caravan down the street to meet with Grant to decide what they were going to do next. Joe took it hard because he was the leader and was under pressure by his militia to have all the answers, but now he didn't.

"Sir, when will you be arriving?" asked Grant over the radio.

"I'll be there in ten minutes," replied Joe over the radio.

"Should I have Johnny and Irina return?"

"Yes, call them now."

Grant took a deep breath as he looked at Sarrjel, "Johnny, come in."

"Yes," replied Johnny over the radio.

"What's your status?"

"We're waiting for your orders," he answered.

"Report to to the first set of stop lights at once down from your street," ordered Grant.

There was a brief silence and a strange sound from Johnny as though he was delaying the action, "we'll be there as soon as we can."

"Something is wrong," whispered Sarrjel.

Grant looked at Sarrjel with a peculiar look, "why, what do you think is wrong?"

"Something happened," said Sarrjel sadly. "I can sense it in his voice."

Deputy stepped into the break room of the library and saw Brenda stuffing her mouth with food, "what the hell are you doing?"

"What does it look like? I'm eating," said Brenda as she talked with her mouth full.

"Did you save me any?" asked Deputy as he walked over to look at the bowel of noodle dish that had a little bit.

"There's some, but right now I'm full," she said.

"Well of course your full now. You didn't leave a brother a meal."

"Well you were on the pot, I wasn't going to knock on your door while your making love to the sink," said Brenda.

"Shut the fuck up," he replied.

Suddenly, the radio buzzed on and it was Grant, "I need you and Brenda to get up here."

"What's the problem?" he asked. "Is everything ok?"

"No problem, just a change in plans."

"Copy that, we're leaving," said Deputy as he nodded at Brenda.

Brenda got up and pet Champ on the head as she followed Deputy out of the break room and out the door.

Grant watched from the stoplight as the caravan arrived from three hundred meters away until it stopped about a foot from Grant. Deputy arrived at the same time with Brenda and Champ and the only squad they were waiting for was Johnny, Irina and Bear.

Joe stepped out of the RV and met with Grant who did a light salute, "what are your orders?"

"I don't know yet," replied Joe.

Suddenly Drone A and B flew up to them from out of nowhere and hovered before them. The two drones had scanned the area outside the perimeters of the squad to watch for enemies.

Sarah came out of the RV from behind and met with everyone who was there followed by Rya and Sara. Suddenly, everyone stopped talking when they heard footsteps and turned around to see it was Johnny and Irina but they looked bloody as though they had been mauled by a tiger. In Johnny's arms was Bear who was limp and near death. Sarrjel closed her eyes in dis-belief.

Johnny laid Bear on the road, "we were ambushed by a creature that looked like a dog. Bear gave his life to us."

"What happened?" asked Joe.

"You didn't go into a house did you?" asked Grant.

"I did," said Irina. "I was tricked."

"What?" said Grant as he looked at Johnny. "I gave you a direct order to not go into the civilian's houses. We don't know who or what is in there."

"Yeah I know," said Johnny.

"It's not his fault. Its all my fault," said Irina as she watched Johnny look sadly at Bear who was on the ground. "I saw children on the lawn and I ran over to them. Then they ran into the house and I followed them. Johnny tried to warn me by yelling my name, but I wouldn't listen. I wanted to save the children."

Sarah walked over to Bear and lowered herself down to look at the wounds and could see large rip marks on his chest and left leg.

"What happened after that?" asked Joe.

"I ran into the house and chased after them down their hallway. Then something tripped and I fell on the carpet. There wasn't much light, but what I saw scared the shit out of me. I saw hundreds of red eyes in the walls looking at me and then something demonic in the wall at the end of the hallway. It stood on all fours and growled at me. Then the children came out from the room that they ran in and revealed themselves and I realized they weren't children at all, but little imps with wings," confirmed Irina.

"What was the beast you saw?" asked Grant.

"I don't know, but it was big, with red fur and glowing red eyes it looked like a wolf. I moved back slowly as I heard wicked laughing, even the children were laughing at me in the most ridiculous high pitch laughter you can imagine. The beast began walking towards me and barked like Bear does except it was deeper in tone. Then I got spooked and ran like hell. I ran out into the living room where there was a lot of light and found myself up against the wall staring at the dog like monster. Then the glass broke and Bear saved my life. He attacked the dog and I watched as the two tried to rip each other apart. Johnny came in with his sub-machine gun shooting at the demons that came out of the walls to attack me, attack us, but they underestimated Johnny," said

Irina as she looked at Johnny and a tear fell on her cheek. Johnny looked to the ground and said nothing, he was humble and self-criticized himself in everything. "Bear and Johnny saved my life."

"We call them hell hounds," said Sarah as she touched Bear's arm and heard him whine in pain. "Easy boy, it'll be ok."

Champ and Shadow walked over to Bear and licked his face and then his wounds. Sarah touched Bear's head and smiled as she hummed to herself.

"Is he going to be alright?" asked Joe.

"He's near death," said Sarah sadly. "He's lost a lot of blood and he's in pain."

"But there's got to be something you can do?" asked Irina as she began to cry. "He saved my life."

Sara started crying and buried her face into Rya's shoulders. Grant looked at Joe and didn't have an answer for him. He gave everyone a direct order to not enter the houses and Irina broke that protocol and they lost a valuable member of the team who was a specially trained police dog.

Then Irina walked up to Sarah who rose up immediately, expecting to get slapped in the face, "I order you to help him, use your magic or your super powers. Bring him back, please," cried Irina who was face to face with Sarah.

"We're not magical fairies or super heroes," said Sarah. "We can only perform small miracles, nothing more."

"Please, please, I beg you don't let him die!" cried Irina as she hesitated. "You're suppose to be angels and heal the sick," she continued and watched Sarah look at Bear and contemplate.

"Alright, I'll try," said Sarah as she kneeled down to pick up Bear with her arms. She walked over to a clear area that was in the middle of the street and closed her eyes. Sarah's wings opened up and a light harmonic sound emanated from her that was similar to the earlier meeting. The sound of morning rain and a light hymn from her voice. Light from the sun formed into a ray and hit her. Minutes passed and suddenly Bear woke up. Sarah opened her eyes and the ray of light stopped just as she stopped hymning. Bear was back on his feet and ran over to Irina and Johnny.

Joe and Grant smiled and were happy to see their friend back from the near death experience. Sarah walked back to the group and stood next to Sarrjel. She looked at Rya and saw Sara and watched Rya smile at her.

Joe, Grant, Johnny, Irina, Brenda, Deputy, Rya , Sara and the angels walked over to the edge of the broken bridge. The German Shepherds stayed behind to be checked over by Mr. Baker, Dallas and Diamond Back. The wind swept through Joe's hair as he bit his lower lip and tried to think of how he was going to get through this.

"Your orders sir?" asked Grant.

"We can't cross it like this. We would need a whole construction crew to work around the clock to fix this so we can drive our caravan through," said Joe as he looked overhead to see the sun shining brightly.

"What do you want to do?" asked Grant.

"We could swim across," said Rya.

"We have about eight inflatable canoes that could carry our people and supplies," said Deputy.

Joe didn't say anything, but made a steady grunting noise as he thought out loud as to what he wanted to do. There had to be a better way, a more direct way to get across the river. Joe turned to the old peninsula that was made into a toll bridge at the end and then looked at Grant.

Grant looked at Joe and then at what he was looking at and expressed interest, "we're talking about building a bridge."

Rya looked at Sara confused just as Sarah and Sarrjel did the same. There was no time to turn back or build anything.

"Joe we must leave this place at once," said Sarrjel.

"Not yet," ordered Joe. "We still have a chance."

"No we don't, we promised our father that we would deliver the boy and you safely to the capital. Johnny sacked the house with demons and they would have given word to Master Scaven. He will be here soon if he isn't already."

"Listen," yelled Joe. "I appreciate what you have done for my people and my dog I really do. You've been good for motivating them and inspiring them to vote for this quest, but I have military equipment that is in a few of those campers, not to mention that they are filled with fuel. My plan is to use as much of my resources as possible and to not give them up to enemy forces especially the Ravens who would use it to power their arsenal."

"You're so sure of yourself," said Sarrjel. "That you need your possessions instead of getting your people out to a safe haven."

"Yes," said Joe as he looked at her with confidence and watched her slowly close her eyes and lower her head out of respect.

Joe turned around and walked back where they came, he used his radio to stay in contact, "Jason, Barry what is the status of the perimeter?"

"Perimeter is clear as far as I know," replied Jason.

"Let me talk to Tim," ordered Joe.

Jason turned his head to look at Tim who was standing over him, "yes Joe."

"How much supplies do we have to extend the toll bridge?"

"We would need heavy steel and rods to fill in the broken space."

"I want you to choose ten men to guard a perimeter of about five-hundred feet," ordered Joe.

When Joe and his squad got back to the caravan he was met with concern by his friend Tim. It wasn't something Joe was expecting and he felt a knot in his stomach.

"Did you carry out my orders?" asked Joe

"Sir, I think there is something you should see," replied Tim as he led Joe and Grant to the sight.

The rest of the crew stood behind, including the angels who weren't interested in watching anymore of Joe's leadership. All seven of the German Shepherds were with about fifteen of the militia squad who were spread out one-hundred feet with different types of machine guns, pistols, M-16 and AR-15 Rifles.

"We can't fix this," said Tim as he showed Joe the old pillars of where the bridge use to be. "Even if we get lucky and put a support system over this shit there's a fucking house in the way on the other side with trees and no road."

"I haven't gone this far just to be held up by this. There has got to be another way," said Joe. "Well sure, if you have a crane and a hundred pounds of cement, but that will attract the Ravens and those demon creatures that invaded our camp."

Joe looked at Grant and shook his head, "this is bull-shit!"

"The only way to get across is to abandon the caravan, take what we need and swim across," said Tim.

"Or we can use a different bridge," said Joe.

"Sir, we spent hours planning this out before we went down here. Driving to a different bridge is fool hearty," said Grant.

Joe thought long and hard, "you guys head back to the caravan I need a few minutes to think."

Grant and Tim walked back to the caravan to meet up with the squad. Everyone was exhausted and their joints ached. Irina was putting hydrogen peroxide on her deep wounds on her chest and scratches on her shoulders from the hell hound that attacked her.

"Are you going to be alright?" asked Dr. Baker as he looked over her hand that was stitched up and bandaged it back up again.

Irina turned her head to look up at the doctor, " yeah, they hurt, but my back hurts the most."

Johnny looked pissed off at Deputy, "fuck this mission! I want to kill some Ravens."

"Fuck you, I want to go to Tahiti with a martini in one hand and a sexy lady in the other," replied Deputy.

"I just don't want to sit here," replied Johnny. "This whole mission is a loss cause."

Grant and Tim walked up the hill to the caravan to figure out a second plan. They saw the squad getting restless and Grant knew he would have to get them in line.

"Hey boss," said Johnny. "Fuck this mission! Can we just attack the Ravens?"

"Not my call, it's up to Joe," replied Grant.

Sarah and Sarrjel had been sitting on the curb across the street and saw the whole thing. They looked at each other and rose up to give council to Joe to see what he wanted to do and to give him good advice to make a good decision.

Joe sat on the bridge supports at the end of the peninsula where the toll bridge was and stared, without blinking, across the twenty feet of open water. He was so close to getting to the other side of the river he could feel it with the edge of his fingers. Now it was gone and it was nothing more than a dream. How could he have been this stupid, why didn't he listen to Grant and follow through with his original plan? Why didn't he send a team to check on the bridge in the first place? Now he would have to abandon his caravan and make way on foot. Walking on foot would make them vulnerable to attacks and it would take even longer to get to the capital. Then suddenly he heard footsteps behind him.

"What's the problem Joe?" asked Sarah.

"Are the waters to deep for you to cross?" asked Sarrjel.

Joe turned around to look at the blonde and black hair guardian angels, "This mission isn't what I expected it to be?"

Sarah and Sarrjel walked over to Joe and sat down next to him on either side. They held both his hands and looked at him with a smile. Joe started to smile and felt a little giddy as his heart began to flutter.

"Crossing the river has been a challenge for explorers for thousands of years and they are willing to do anything to breach it," said Sarrjel.

"Anything?" asked Joe.

"Anything," said Sarah.

Joe looked at them both and pushed their hands away from his, "why are you here ? I thought you were Rya's good luck charm."

"What?" asked Sarrjel.

"What's a good luck charm?" asked Sarah.

"Don't you belong to Rya?" asked Joe as he looked at both of them.

"We don't belong to anyone," said Sarah.

"We belong to our father," began Sarrjel. "Just as you belong to Him."

"I thought I had freewill?" asked Joe. "You do," said Sarah. "But Satan will make you believe you have no choice or will of your own and demand servitude but our Father loves you and loves all. He wants all of us to come home and you always have a choice."

"When I first met you. I prejudged you and I'm sorry," said Joe

"Yes, we understand," said Sarrjel. "It'll be ok and it'll pass."

"There is one thing I want to know. I saw those men shoot you with their bullets and they didn't' hurt you. So when you came to the camp, why did you act in fear? The bullets wouldn't hurt or kill you?"

"We are angels and have limits to our power. We can be hurt by bullets if we are not conscious to them hitting us. We can be killed if we're not prepared and if it's a powerful weapon. We are blessed with our father to receive strength from all or to give strength and life to one. We are not invincible to take on multiple bullets or blades into our body," said Sarrjel as she smiled and watched Joe look at her with admiration.

"We could help with your problem," said Sarah.

Joe looked at Sarah with a peculiar look, "how?"

"We could lift the water and clear the trees," said Sarah.

"Can you do that?"

"Of course," said Sarah. "Time is short and we need to get to the capital within the hour."

"You would have to find a way to get your caravan up the steep hill," said Sarrjel.

Joe looked at them both and then got up to scratch his head, "well then let's go."

"We will need time to find the right path through the river bed,"said Sarrjel.

"What?" he asked.

"The river bed isn't smooth," added Sarah.

"Fine," said Joe as he got excited and began to walk back with confidence and assurance that they wouldn't be leaving the caravan behind.

When Joe got back to the caravan he met with Grant, "radio in the rest of the militia. We're getting out of here."

"What's going on?" asked Grant.

"I'll tell you in a minute," said Joe. "As soon as we get everyone here."

Sarah and Sarrjel stared into the river and waited for the militia to gather. They were looking deep into the water with their eyes to see the best spot to create a path. Then Rya walked up to them to see what they were doing.

"What's going on?"

"We're looking into the water," said Sarrjel.

"Are we going to create a bridge to get across?"

Sarrjel looked at Sarah and then back at Rya, "we're making a path through the water."

"What?"

"Moses asked our Father to raise the sea and we're doing the same," said Sarrjel.

"Time is short and things are not so simple," said Sarah.

"This I got to see," said Rya with a smile.

Then the militia showed up with Joe leading them to the edge of the river near the peninsula of the toll bridge. They seemed interested in what was going on and didn't want to waste anytime. The angels turned around to face them just as Rya joined with Sara. They felt uncomfortable because of the expression on the militia's faces.

"We have a plan to get across the river," began Joe. "It's going to involve a lot of hard work, but it beats walking twenty miles to the capital."

"What's going on?" asked Diamond Back.

Joe looked at the two guardian angels, "pitch it."

"We're going to cross the river in a few minutes and move the trees, but it's up to you to get your heavy trucks and motor homes up the rugged terrain,"

"Excuse me, what are you talking about?" asked Deputy.

61

"We will move the water so you can cross," said Sarrjel. "We have the power bestowed upon us by our Father to grant small miracles."

"That's a pretty big miracle," said Brenda. "Why don't you just teleport us to the capital and save us the trouble."

"Teleport?" asked Sarrjel confused. "What is that?"

"Things are not so simple," said Sarah.

"Why don't you just make us walk on water?" asked Deputy. "I'd love to experience that."

Sarah and Sarrjel looked at each other confused and then back at the militia. Sarah looked at Rya and smiled as she turned around to follow Sarrjel to the river. When they got to the river their wings spread open and their arms opened up. Rya watched closely but couldn't see their faces, but he knew something was happening. Suddenly, the clouds began to move and it became dark. The wind started to pick up and was moving at about fifty miles an hour.

Joe turned to Grant, "let's get the heavy trucks moving. I want cables and hydraulic lifts ready to pull our shit up that hill."

"Yes sir," said Grant as he led the way.

Right away the militia got mobilized and ran back to the caravan to get moving. Sarrjel and Sarah moved into the water and it went up to their knees. They had their mouths open and their eyes began to glow white as a strange high pitch noise emanated from their vocal cords. A strange purple and bluish color moved throughout their wings, suddenly a burst of lighting struck them both and the two angels moved their hands and arms apart as though they were ripping a fabric apart and the water began to move. It moved from the bottom of the channel to form a twenty foot wide path.

Sara's mouth dropped as she watched in disbelief, "look at that!"

Rya looked as well and couldn't believe his eyes, "wow they're actually doing it."
The two angels walked to the end of the channel and concentrated on the trees in front of them. They had hymned loudly and reached the ahs and hes and um as they're eyes were brightly colored in white light. The trees in front of the path suddenly burst into ash and fell apart.

The way was clear and the angels moved aside as Joe led the way with his trucks and campers. He shifted it into four-wheel drive and climbed up the steep slop on the river bed and up the hill where the trees were. He made it and got out to clamp a heavy duty cable to a large oak tree that wasn't in the way. Then he waited for the rest of the caravan to come and stop. The militia worked together to strap on cables and hydraulic lifts to the frame of every motor home and RV that was not going to make it on it's own.   Most of the Jeeps were able to make it up the steep terrain of the river bed and up the hill. It was hard work and all fifty of the militias pushed the campers up the steep hill and terrain until everyone of them were out of the way. The angels walked from the channel all the way up to the disintegrated trees with their arms and hands up in the air and their eyes brighter than the brights of a car at night. Once their arms lowered and their eyes glowed and then dimmed the water clashed back into the channel. It splashed hard like a monster and the militia watched in shock as they heard the loud clash of water splashing into each other.

"I can't believe we made it," said Joe.

Sarrjel turned to him, "now that we have made it, we must leave at once to the capital. Everything depends on it."

"What time are we suppose to be there?" asked Joe.

"We must be there at five o'clock. Five means change and was given to us by our Father to escort you to salvation, said Sarah. "We spent two hours getting you across the river and up the hill. Now we ask you to take care in your efforts to the capital."

Joe turned to his militia, "let's get moving!"

The militia continued the journey on highway forty-nine. Joe was driving the RV and leading his people to the capital and had to slow down to drive around cars and pieces of debris that ranged from large rocks to pillars and even pieces of aircraft.

"I can't believe I'm seeing this," said Sara sadly as she stood up and looked through the windshield to see the destruction of what was left behind.

Rya looked at his girlfriend sadly, "it's just material that is lost. We still have each other."

"Yes, but a few weeks ago, everything was fine and people were in their cars going to work. Today I saw dead bodies laying on the side of the road. Children were burnt and lying lifeless. How can I forget this?" asked Sara.

"This world isn't real," said Sarah. "Only the Kingdom of God is real, that which you bring inside yourselves."

Joe didn't say anything and was concentrating on the road. He was tired and his body hurt from all the running around that he had been doing as well as pushing and pulling the vehicles up the rugged terrain. Then suddenly he felt someone put their hands on the back of his neck. He turned his head to see it was Sarrjel and she smiled at him.

"We're almost there," said Joe.

"Your tired," replied Sarrjel.

Joe continued to drive and concentrated on the road, "I'm exhausted."

"Take your worries of the day and give them to me," said Sarrjel as she began to massage his neck and shoulders.

Almost immediately, Joe felt a surge of energy come over him and before he knew it they were pulling off to the exit ramp to head to the capital from one street to the next.

Sarrjel took her hands off of Joe as they pulled into the parking lot. The entire caravan had pulled off in different parking areas to wait for Joe's orders.

Joe got up from the driver's seat and stood up. He turned around to look straight at Sarrjel who then backed away to let him pass.

"Thank you for what you did," said Joe as he looked at her, "the river I mean."

Sarrjel looked at him and smiled, "I only did what would help us."

"Opening up the river and clearing the trees takes some power to endure," continued Joe as he walked past to walk out the door.

Sarrjel turned her head to look at him while his back was turned, "only compared to some."

Joe stopped for a second but didn't turn to look at her and continued to walk out of the RV to meet with his militia. Rya took Sara's hand and led her outside. Sarah and Sarrjel followed until they were out the door.

Fifteen minutes passed and everyone was getting restless. Sarah and Sarrjel sat down on the stairs at the capital with Rya and Sara to wait for the meeting.

Rya looked at his watch and it was a few minutes after four o'clock, "so where is our ride?"

The angels looked at Rya and began to laugh. They looked at each other while laughing and then back at him.

"The ride is coming," said Sarah with a grin.

Joe watched the angels laugh and talk to Rya and then turned to Grant, "I want every square inch of this capital checked out. Get two search parties to march around the building. Something doesn't seem right."

"Yes sir," said Grant and he snapped his finger and gestured for Johnny, Deputy, Jason, Barry, Irina, Brenda, George and Dallas to join him.

"We'll split up into teams and check out the perimeter of the capital. We get back here in fifteen minutes," ordered Grant.

"Jason, Irina, Deputy and George you are team one. Team two will be lead by me Barry, Johnny, Brenda and Dallas. You guys take the northern section and we'll take the southern part, said Grant.

The two teams moved out quickly to cover more ground in a timely fashion. Joe watched them and looked towards the road that led into the parking lot. They were a sitting duck with no way to escape if the Raven army moved in with the demons. The last action they had was the RVs and the campers with loaded fuel tanks that could be used in their last line of defense, to set off explosions.

Minutes passed and the sun set over the horizon. The two angels began to pace as they waited and Rya was becoming restless.

"Sarah, what's going on?" he asked.

Sarah looked at Sarrjel and then back at Rya, "I don't know, my orders were to bring you to the capital and wait for further instructions."

"Wait for further instructions!" yelled Sara. "What are you a robot?"

Sarah didn't say anything and could see that she was upset. She had every right to be because they trusted them and now they were feeling betrayed. Then suddenly Sarah turned to see the militia walking towards them led by Joe and Grant.

"We surveyed this whole location and there's nobody here," said Joe. "Where is your contact?"

Sarah hesitated as she looked uncomfortable and stammered, "I don't know."

"You don't know or you don't want to tell us!" yelled George. "They're lying to us . They've lied to us from the beginning."

"We didn't lie to you," said Sarrjel.

"Well you told us that there was going to be someone here," said Deputy.

"I said you would reach salvation if you traveled with us to the capital."

"Well what difference does that make? We're the fools sitting on our asses waiting for something that isn't coming," said Deputy.

"I hear something coming," said Sarrjel. "In Hustle by the bridge."

Joe turned to Grant, "Get the two big guns ready and armed."

"Yes sir," said Grant as he ran back to the campers.

Joe turned to Jason and Barry, " I want you to, to get the drones up and running and find out who we're up against."

Jason and Barry wasted no time and made a run for the camper with the monitor and remote technology. Joe turned his head back to the guardian angels and shook his head, "I should have expected this. We were better off going to Marshfield."

Sarah looked at Joe and could sense hostility from him, "I'm sorry."

"Your sorry? That's all you got to say? Do you know where you put us?" asked Joe.

"No, I don't," said Sarah.

"You put us in harms way, that's what you did," replied Joe as he left to try and prepare for an attack.

"Joe, stop!" yelled Sarrjel.

Joe halted and turned around to look at the black haired angel, "what?"

"You and your militia must come in closer to the capital for cover," she commanded.

"Really, is that right?" began Joe with a peculiar look. "Is that an order or a request?"

"Joe," began Sarrjel. "It's not safe by your campers and vehicles. Bring your weapons here at the capital where you can hide behind the pillars and stone walls."

An Angel's Whisper

Joe looked at the angel and walked away with the remainder of his militia to get set up.

Suddenly, Sarah was visited by the little bird that she talked to earlier today, before they left on their journey. She held the bird gently in her hands and heard what it had to say. Then her eyes widened in fear, "Master Scaven is coming."

An hour passed and the drones flew in the direction of the freeway to see what Sarrjel heard. The militia armed heavily, carrying as much as they could handle. They set up booby traps about twenty feet around the capital and the vehicles were parked slanted and apart. Many of them were gutted out of technologies and were a mere shell.

Joe watched Dallas and Tim put the German Shepherds under hypnosis with their machine. All seven of the smart dogs were ready to protect, the militia.

Dallas and Tim both spoke in German to instruct the dogs to be selfless and protect the militia and to kill their enemies. Champ, Shadow and Bear were already on duty before, but the new smart dogs like Thunder, Duke, Empire and Lady had not seen as much action as the other three.

"Stay here at the capital," warned Sarah. "You will both be safe here."

Sarrjel walked down to where the campers were and the militia was getting ready to fight. Sarah walked quickly to join Sarrjel so she could witness what was going on.

"Sarrjel, I received word that Master Scaven will be here," said Sarah

"Then we will fight him," said Sarrjel.

"Yes, but we can't beat him," whispered Sarah. "We're not strong enough."

"We will do what we must," said Sarrjel. "Jesus will protect us."

Rya stayed where he was with Sara and watched them leave and talk to Joe. He was worried about everyone including the angels and hoped that everything would be ok.

"What's going on?" asked Sarrjel.

"We just saw on the laptop that the drones found an army of the Ravens marching on the streets about two-hundred meters from here and they'll be here within the hour," said Jason as he turned from the laptop monitor and looked at the angels. "Maybe even sooner."

"Any idea how they crossed the river?" asked Joe.

"I don't know," said Sarrjel.

Sarah and Sarrjel watched on the monitor to see about two-hundred men dressed in army and riot gear and ranged in all sizes. Sarah also could see demons marching and flying above the raven army with the company of two hell hounds. One of the hell hounds looked beaten up.

"You can't win this battle," said Sarrjel.

"No," began Joe. "But with your help we may have a chance."

Sarrjel looked at Sarah and then at Joe, "we didn't come here to fight battles. We came here to protect."

Joe looked at Sarrjel with disappointment before leaving to prepare for battle. He was met with Grant who was stalked up with firearms and an AR-15 in his hands.

"Sir, I highly recommend we get in our caravan and make a run for it."

"Where are we going to go?" asked Joe. "Who's going to save us ? We're sitting ducks. The only way to get out is through the broken bridge area and we know that isn't going to happen. The other bridge is up in the town of Water Still and the one near Taylor Town is about a two hour drive near Otter Township. We don't know if those bridges are intact," continued Joe as he loaded both his sub-machine guns and his M-16.

"So we're fighting to the death, sir?" asked Grant.

"I guess so," said Joe as he put both guns over his shoulders by their sling. "Better to die on our feet than our knees."

Suddenly, both men stopped when they saw Tim ride in on his motorcycle. He got off his bike and took off his helmet as he marched to Joe, "sir they'll be here in ten minutes."

Joe looked at Tim adamantly and then at Grant and yelled, "everybody arm yourselves and take your positions. Ellis, Connie and Marge and the other mothers walked over to Joe with about eight-teen children and teenagers.

"We can't have them here or they'll be killed," said Ellis.

Before Joe could speak Sarrjel cut in, "I'll take the children up to the capital where they'll be safe."

Ellis looked at the angel with distrust, "how do we know they'll be safe? You already lied about us getting help."

"I give you my word the children will be safe and help will come, I promise you," said Sarrjel.

Joe turned to Sarrjel and then back at Ellis and nodded his head to assure her it was ok. Ellis looked at Sarrjel and then directed the children to go with Sarah who led them back to the capital where Sara and Rya were.

The militia waited for the Raven Army and every minute that passed felt like a life time. Their faces were marked up to match the green and gray camouflage uniform. They kept in contact by radio.

"Everyone report in," ordered Joe.

"Grant reporting in."

"Deputy reporting in."

"Johnny reporting in."

"Brenda reporting in."

"Irina reporting in."

"Dallas reporting in."

"Dallas are you in position to see the Raven's drawing close?" asked Joe.

"Yes sir, I'm on top of the bell tower at the church across the street."

The rest of the militia reported in and Joe watched through his binoculars to see black Jeeps roll in the area and an army of figures dressed in black outfits with helmets that had visors over their faces. Joe noticed that some of the figures were about nine or ten feet tall and were big. The large figures were dressed the same way as the smaller figures that were around six feet in height. They all had machine guns in their hands and it was difficult to know if they had more weapons, but the outfits looked rubbery and stiff.

Suddenly, there was a large black Hummer that rolled up the lot where the campers were and it stopped. Twenty more black Jeeps rolled up with about eight soldiers inside with a mounted machine gun. The militia took positions behind rocks, cars, debris and the children had been led to hide behind the pillars by the stairs of the capital. George, Diamond Back and Mr. Baker as well as Deputy stood next to Grant at the stone wall that was three feet in height and watched his guardian angels stand next to Joe behind a Jeep near the edge of the perimeter to protect him. Rya and Sara had little gun training and were only given pistols to protect themselves. The seven German Shepherds were spread apart with the militias and watched patiently for the time to attack.

Champ was with Joe and his tongue panted as he waited for the command. Shadow and Bear were next to Grant near the capital grounds and were waiting patiently the command to be given by Grant. As the Hummer waited for several minutes a Jeep suddenly pulled up in front of the Raven army and Joe recognized the man as General Hex who he had seen on TV before the attack, a few weeks ago. There were two other important people in business suits that looked like twins and well armed officers in Kevlar.

Just then hundreds of small demon imps flew towards the Jeeps and then landed. They made high pitch noises like birds and squeals that sounded like a pig. They were dark and leathery with no clothes. Their eyes had a red iris and their ears were pointy like their teeth. When they saw Sarrjel by the parked Jeep with Joe they made loud high pitch snarls and screeches that were agonizing to hear.

Forty large demons that ranged from five feet to six feet flew in and landed next to the Raven army ready to fight and were armed with small daggers, swords and guns. Two hell hounds emerged through the crowd next to one of the largest demons and glared at the angels and the German Shepherd. One of the hell hounds looked like it had been attacked by another animal.

Bear recognized the hell hound that he had fought to protect Irina from and began to growl and then barked aggressively. Shadow began to growl to, but kept his place.

"Easy boy," whispered Grant as he pet Bear's head. "Let it go."

A man stepped out of the Hummer with two body guards at his side. The marching army closed in at the spot where the Hummer was and the man who stepped out, looked around. He was a good looking man who was known by everyone in the USA and the rest of the world.

"No fucking way," said Johnny.

"Is that the anti-Christ?" asked Irina over the radio.

Joe closed his eyes in dis-belief and knew who it was and replied over the radio, "no it's the President of the United States."

President Kran was handed a loudspeaker by one of his business associate. Just before he was going to speak into it, Master Scaven glided down with his leathery bat like wings spread open and then folded back into a cape.

Master Scaven was one of the Master's most formidable servants to be feared. He was seven feet tall with a large build and carried a large black sword with red rubies on the handle. He wore a gold tunic around his waist and jewelry such as a gold ring and necklace. His skin was a lavender color with scales on his torso. He had a muscular chest like a body builder, long brown hair and green eyes. Most demons had red eyes, but Master Scaven had green eyes. They were given to him from a psychic woman who worked with dark energy and knew too much about their plan.

Sarrjel looked at Master Scaven and tried to hide her fear of him. He was known as the angel killer by the other angels and almost none of the lower archangels could kill him one on one because he was strong and skilled in his slights of fighting dirty.

"Sarrjel!" yelled the demon as he began to walk towards her.

"Master Scaven!" yelled the president. "I didn't give the order to attack yet!"

Master Scaven ignored him and kept walking towards her, "I got a bitch to kill."

"Master Scaven!" yelled General Hex. "You gave your word to the master that you would follow the president's orders."

Master Scaven stopped ten feet from Sarrjel, Joe and Champ. He watched the German Shepherd growl and snarl at him and Joe cocked his pistol with his hand as it rested in its holster. Sarrjel stared at him and was waiting for him to make his move. She could feel his hatred towards her and her stomach tightened. Master Scaven turned his head to the president and General Hex.

"But she needs to die! That little bitch has killed more of my brothers than I can count. She deserves to die!" he exclaimed.

"She will die, but not until we negotiate," said General Hex.

"Desist and return," ordered President Kran.

"Just remember you're fucking dead, you little bitch," whispered Master Scaven to Sarrjel as he turned around to walk back to the demon and Raven army.

"What the hell was that all about?" whispered Joe.

Sarrjel took a deep breath, "it's complicated. Long story short he is angry that I injured Malicious and sent him away like a coward. I also have killed many of his subordinates and he knows who I am."

"Militia," began President Kran. "I'm asking you to stand down, surrender yourselves to the Raven Army and the Nation United."

"Why should we do that?" yelled Joe.

"I'm sorry can you tell us who you are?"

"My name is Joseph Warren and I'm the leader of the Zion Outpost of the Western Wisconsin Militia."

"Joseph, surrender yourselves to the United States. What you're doing is considered terrorism. If you surrender now you will be treated fairly and given a new life," said President Kran.

"Yeah right!" yelled Joe. "The conduct you have been doing is terrorism. You were responsible for breaking the constitution, destroying freedom and liberty and taking away our future!"

"I give you my word. If you give up your guns and your ammunition. You will be treated fairly," said President Kran. "If you do not surrender you will be taken by force. We will have to fire upon you and many of your friends will die. Your loved ones will be saddened by your death. Is that what you want?" asked President Kran with a sad tone in his voice.

Sarrjel whispered into Joe's ear, "he's lying. He will never give you a new life. It's a trick to get you to fall into his trap. He'll take each of you one by one into camps and de-program you to live by Satan in a world of lies. Remember, Jesus once said that this world is ruled under a lie and Satan means liar and deceiver."

"What should we do?" he whispered.

"You'll have to fight," she whispered as she looked at Joe and then back at the army.

Joe turned his head back to the capital where his militia were hidden and Dallas watched with his binoculars to see hand signals which told everyone to prepare for battle and for Dallas to shoot the machine gun at the standing army so that he could escape.

"Now it's for all our best interest to live in a world of peace and harmony," continued the president. "We can have the nice house, two door garage, good job, two kids and wife with the white picket fence. This is something we have worked hard for all our lives, but we can't have it if we have people in this world that have this idea of capitalism, greed and self-indulgence. This world is dying and needs us to take care of it. We can't have people living out in the country and commuting into the cities while polluting the Earth. We need everyone to give up this idea of possessions and lease the things that they adhere to. We need everyone to live in the city. The city life isn't that bad, you'll see. What do you say Joseph? I'll offer you five-hundred million dollars if you give up your gun and come with me. I'll sign a written contract to pay you and let you live like a king."

The president looked at Joseph and waited for him to answer. Sarrjel looked at Master Scaven and watched a grin emerge as Joe was tempted for the money. The president smiled as did General Hex.

"What do you say? Will you accept my deal?" asked President Kran.

"From my cold dead hands," said Joe.

"What? What does that mean?" asked the president.

"Don't tread on me!"

President Krans looked at Joe with a distasteful expression on his face. He gesture for General Hex to come to him and Master Scaven.

"Get ready," whispered Sarrjel as she gripped her sword.

Joe turned his head and made another hand signal to Dallas in the tower. Dallas took his flash light and turned it on and off to let Joe know that he was in position and was going to open fire on their location. Joe then hand signaled to the other teams to get ready to fire.

"I don't care what you got to do," whispered the president to General Hex. "I want those people dead. This is going to end in bloodshed no matter what and that mother fucker with the winged freak is mocking me."

"Understood," said General Hex as he was just going to turn around with Master Scaven.

"No, not you," said President Kran.

"What?" growled the demon.

"I need you here to protect me. Yeah, the one man those terrorist are going to shoot is going to be me and I can tell you right now I'm very important and can't be replaced," declared the president.

"But I want to kill Sarrjel."

"Trust me there will be plenty of time for that," said General Hex. "Stay here to protect the President of the United States."

Master Scaven began to grumble after a deep growl, " I don't believe this bull-shit."

"I'll kill Sarrjel Master Scaven," said a voice.

The trio turned to look at the demon as he moved through the crowd of demons. He had recovered from his wounds and wanted revenge with the two angels that had humiliated him.

"Malicious you have healed," said Master Scaven.

"Yes my lord and I want the honor to kill Sarrjel."

"Very well, but don't disappoint me."

Master Scaven took his place next to the president and nodded to Malicious. General Hex left the president with Malicious and said something to his lieutenant. Suddenly, the army quickly pulled out their guns and aimed at Joe and Sarrjel, but before they open fired Dallas fired his machine gun from on top of the tower and mowed the demon, nephilim and Raven Army down like grass.

Tim fired his RPG Missile launcher from behind the pillar near the capital on the right side at the Raven Army. Johnny fired a missile from behind a camper on the left side of the capital and the Raven Army scattered to take cover as they fired at the militia who drew their guns and fired. Joe and the angel made a run for it behind a Jeep and watched as body parts could be seen all over the ground from the missiles. Smoke and dust from the explosion rose up to the sky, making it hard to see. The demons flew in all different directions and tried to attack the militia but were shot down by the militia. One after the other fell to their death. Sarrjel pulled out her sword and shot lightning at the imps that were charging after them. Each small demon screamed in a high pitch squeal as they blew apart into pieces of flesh.

Dallas continued to fire his big machine gun from on top of the tower building. He was aiming at the Raven Army as they were running and taking cover behind trees, bushes and turned over cars on the streets. They stopped firing their guns at the militia on the ground and aimed their guns at Dallas.

Suddenly, about fifty imp demons flew at Dallas and he quickly raised his machine gun at them to fire when he heard something behind him. Dallas turned his head quickly to see it was Brenda and Tim. They smiled at him before looking at each other.

"What the hell are you doing here?" asked Dallas.

"Saving your ass!" yelled Tim as he helped Dallas kill the flying imp demons that were charging at them with his AR-15 Rifle.

Joe and Sarrjel made a run for the camper with Duke a long side them to take cover. The Raven Army was shooting at them and came close to taking down Joe. Joe turned and fired from his machine gun at the Raven Army.

Sarah watched from a distance to see where Sarrjel was but couldn't see her. She used her special ability of seeing through the dust and her hearing until she could hear her voice.

"Is everything ok?" asked Rya.

Before Sarah could answer, a huge number of imp demons led by larger sized demons in height flew at them like a flock of birds. Sarah quickly pulled out her sword and struck each of them one after the other. A dozen of the bigger humanoid demons presented a challenge. Sarah swung her sword with grace at the bigger demons who had swords or spears in their hands.

"Take the children and run to the inside of the capital!" yelled Sarah.

Rya took Sara's hand and they gathered the children to make a run for it. Sarah moved out of the way from a charging demon with his sword and decapitated his head.

Grant fired his M2 machine gun at the charging Raven Army made up of nephilims. They carried the same machine guns and fired thousands of bullets at him and his team on the pillar just before the capital.

"Oh shit!" yelled Grant as he ducked under the shield of his big gun.

"What the fuck kind of body armor are those assholes wearing?" yelled Deputy.

"Shoot them with the bazooka!" ordered Grant.

Deputy raised the bazooka and aimed in the center of the small complement army of giants. Grant continued to fire his M2-Browning .50 caliber machine gun at each nephilim and noticed that if he concentrated his fire power he could kill them one at a time.

Deputy fired his Bazooka and the missile struck the Nephilim in the center of the group and blew him apart and severely injured almost the whole group from the explosion of bullets.

"Yeah!" yelled Deputy as he gave Grant a high five but their cheers were short lived when one of the Nephilim was seen aiming his M20 Rocket Launcher at them, but before the giant pulled the trigger he saw in the distance Rya and Sara making a run for the inside of the capital. The Nephilim smiled and pulled the trigger and the missile shot out and headed towards Grant's position.

"Get down, get down, get down!" yelled Grant to his team but the missile flew over them and struck the capital building.

"Get back!" yelled Rya as he retreated from the falling rock and debris.

Sara picked up one of the youngest children and made a run back as the debris nearly collapsed on all of them. After a minute, when the dust settled Rya saw that the entrance inside was blocked and there was nowhere to go.

The nephilim moved up his face visor and smiled until a bullet shot into his throat and then another one into his mouth. The giant looked to see where the two bullets came from and it was from Joe.

"You have to get out of here," said Sarrjel.

"We leave together," said Joe with a light smile.

Just then a small army of demons emerged through the dust and were carrying, machine guns, swords, morning stars, morning star flails and spears. The demons charged after Sarrjel and Joe, but were attacked by Johnny and Irina with their machine guns. Thunder, Duke and Empire also charged next to their masters, but didn't fight until they were called for. Champ barked violently at the demons that Sarrjel had killed swiftly one after the other until she came face to face with Malicious.

"It's been a long time, Sarrjel," said the demon slowly.

"Not nearly long enough," replied the guardian angel.

"Where do you think you're going?"

Sarrjel didn't answer and only looked at Joe, "get out of here Joe. Get your men out of here and take Rya home."

"But we can kill him with gun fire."

"No," said Sarrjel. "It's not the angel way. In honor and in God, we fight for honesty and fairness."

Malicious began to laugh at her, "that's how I was able to beat you last time because you're weak."

"You never beat me," began Sarrjel. "I cut you and nearly killed you."

"You were lucky," replied malicious, "but this time I will kill you."

Joe nodded and looked at Johnny, "let's get back for cover."

"But sir the entrance is blocked," said Johnny. "We can't get inside."

Joe looked at Sarrjel, "we'll find a way. Let's get going!"

"I'll take care of Malicious," said Sarrjel as she turned her eyes from Joe to the demon.

"Take care of me? How are you going to take care of me. I'll be taking care of you when I cut off your head and sell it on the black market."

General Hex watched the destruction of their small army that was supposed to have taken out the small rebellion. He let out a deep sigh as the two men in business men in suits walked up to him. They were twins and looked identical with their black sunglasses and expensive black and white suits.

"The Illuminati doesn't accept failure."

"Mr. Gray we're doing our best."

"It's not good enough," said the other man.

"What would you have me do Mr. Black?"

"Do better, kill the angel and the militia. Our council doesn't allow failure on our clock," replied Mr. Black.

General Hex looked at President Kran who spoke up, "send in our second wave with the predator drones."

Master Scaven looked at General Hex with a disdain look on his face and then looked away. General Hex turned to his Lieutenant and nodded as he looked ahead to the capital of St. Paul.

"Call in the second wave and two predator drones!" exclaimed General Hex.

Sarah had just finished off the last demon by chopping off his head. The humanoid demon's head rolled on the ground and she quickly turned around to aid Rya, but found them twenty feet ahead and they were stopped by the rubble in front of the entrance of the capital. A few of the militia members showed up to help and Sarah felt a sense of relief, but she still needed to hold out a little longer.

"The entrance is blocked," said Rya. "What are we going to do?"

"Have patience and faith," said Sarah. "All we have to do is wait."

"What's going on down there?" asked Deputy as he pulled out his binoculars.

Grant squinted his eyes to see what was going on, "it looks like they're leaving, but the angel is staying behind to give them cover."

Deputy got up and was leaving until Grant raised his voice, "hey where are you going?"

"She saved my life and I'm not going to let her fight those things by herself."

Shadow and Bear began to growl and whine as they looked at Grant for his command, but received none. They were anxious to help out their brother Champ, but weren't given an order.

Dallas noticed all the imp demons were retreating , "yes we won. Now hopefully they'll leave."

"Uh don't count on it," said Tim. "They're up to something."

"I got a bad feeling about this," said Brenda. "I think we should get the hell out of here."

Dallas turned to look at them, "do you hear something?"

There was a strange motor noise that sounded like a lawn mower in the distance. Dallas quickly looked over his artillery to see he had a thousand rounds and cocked his gun to get ready to fire.

Sarah heard the same sound as well and looked around to see where it was coming from. She became fearful and her heart began to beat faster as she realized it was something that could fly.

"What is that?" asked Rya.

"Stay here," commanded Sarah as she walked back to the edge of the fenced in area. Her eyes widened when she saw Sarrjel facing off against Malicious and about twenty demons were waiting to attack.

"What is she doing?" whispered Sarah in anger and confused.

Barry and Jason could hear the noise as they stayed at their post and looked around for whatever it was. They held their sub-machine guns tightly until Barry saw something with his binoculars.

"What do you see?" asked Jason.

Barry saw another wave of about one-hundred men marching up the street with a couple of black Jeeps that had huge machine guns on the back, equipped with a bullet proof shield. nephilims could be seen marching alongside regular men in black, armored outfits with army caps. The nephilim were carrying M1 and M2 machine guns and others were carrying missile launchers M-20s. A cloud of imp demons hovered above them and were moving towards the capital.

"We're in deep shit," said Barry as he looked at Jason. "They're sending everything they got."

Two objects appeared in the sky that looked like fighter jets, but as they got closer they were smaller and had what looked like the head of a bird on the beak of the plane. There was two of them and they split up to cover more area.

The first predator drone stood about ten feet in front of Sarrjel and a high powered machine gun popped out from below and open fired to strike the angel down. Sarrjel used her sword to block every bullet as fast as she could for several minutes. Joe and the others made a run for it to escape. Johnny covered them and took the rear.

The predator drone then stopped and flew away. Sarrjel watched it fly towards the capital and turned around to fight the demons that were charging at her. Malicious pulled out his sword and swung as he charged. The demons used their assortment of weapons to try to kill her but ended up hitting air. A demon with the morning star hit Sarrjel's sword and heard the sound of a clang and was quickly taken back as she moved her sword from it's position to cut the demon's fore-arm. Malicious caught her sword with his and licked his lips as he quickly moved in to strike her down.

"Go after the militia and kill them!" commanded Malicious to the demons.

The predator drone flew towards Grant's position and open fired on him while he fired his big machine gun. The drone then locked in on the target and fired a missile. Grant looked at his two German Shepherds and moved his hand quickly for them to make a run for it. He leaped out of the way with the dogs just as the missiles struck the gun and blew it up. Grant took a deep breath and a sigh of relief and held his AR-15 in his hand. Shadow and Bear whined and licked his face to show their affection for their master.

"Hey, I'm ok," said Grant with a light laugh and smile.

Sarah watched the predator drone fly towards her, but before she was able to attack she saw Ellis with her son Erike running for cover. The little boy that she met earlier and the drone turned to them and open fired before Sarah could save them. Ellis stood in front of her son with her back turned and kneeled down to cover Erike. Sarah screamed in anger and ran over to see if she could help her.

The predator drone could see Sarah and was going to shoot her but saw the group of children with Rya and Sara and decided to shoot them instead because there were more targets. Rya could hear the sound of machine gun fire, grabbed Sara as fast as he could to make a run for it to the edge of the building. A flame thrower engaged from the bottom of the drone, next to the machine gun and shot a fifty foot stream of fire from it's flame thrower unit and burned all the children alive. Sarah could hear them screaming in pain and rose up quickly with her sword from Ellis and Erike. Her wings opened up as she raised her sword in the air to charge her energy. Her wings began to glow white and then blue with a tint of purple as she jumped up with her sword and split the drone in half. Sarah was so angry and had raised enough energy to take on the whole army.

After about ten minutes Sarah calmed down and walked back to Ellis and kneeled down to look at her. She was hoping that Erike was still alive. Ellis was dead and when Sarah turned her over she saw that Erike was dead to. The stillness in his eyes said it all and the bullet wound in the head showed how he died. Sarah sniffled and cried as she held him.

"I am so sorry Ellis," cried Sarah. "I failed to save you and your son."

"You were so young," she balled. "You didn't deserved to leave so soon."

Rya opened his eyes to see he was ok. He was laying on the pavement, but Sara wasn't next to him.

"Sara!" he yelled.

"It's ok," said a feminine voice.

Rya turned around to see Sara in front of him. She had been shot in the back and the bullet went out her chest.

"No it's ok," she repeated as she suddenly fell forward onto his lap.

"Sara!" yelled Rya as he got up quickly and tried to stop the bleeding.

Sarah turned her head and saw that Rya's girlfriend had been shot and was dying. There was nothing that she could do to save her because she didn't have enough power. Sarah looked ahead at the fire fight below and the marching nephilim with machine guns and missile launchers and knew what she had to do. Her eyes began to pulse white as she re-assessed her anger. He sword began to glow white like lighting and she took to the air with the movement of her wings.

The militia fired their guns at the charging demons and took them out one by one, but then when the nephilim showed up with their machine guns and opened fired they found themselves scrambling to escape. The nephilims that carried missile launchers fired and there was an endless mess of explosions and dust in the air. Grant tried to see what was ahead, but couldn't see five feet in front of him. All of a sudden a hell hound jumped through the haze of dust that looked like smoke and Grant could see the beast's glowing red eyes and red fur coat as it snarled. It knocked the wind out of him and grabbed his arm, but before it could rip it off Bear and Shadow barked violently and attacked the hell hound which released Grant's arm. Grant squinted his eyes to watch the two German Shepherds attack the hell hound aggressively by clamping their jaws onto the hell hound's neck and fore-arm and shook their head quickly until the hell hound cried in pain and managed to shake both the German Shepherds off before running away yelping like crazy.

Bear and Shadow walked over to their master and licked their lips. They were both wounded in the chest and back, but they were ok. Grant took a deep breath and sighed in relief.

"Protect," he said.

Shadow began to growl and then barked just as Bear did.

"Protect Joe! Go now!" commanded Grant.

Both of the German Shepherds turned and made a run like no other to find and protect their brother Champ and their other master, Joe.

"You should have kept the dogs here, piece of shit!" yelled a masculine gruffy voice.

Grant quickly turned his head to see a demon walk towards him with a morning star and swung it as fast as he could. Grant pulled out his gun and tried to shoot the beast, but the demon struck and busted the the M-15 into pieces.

Grant screamed in pain as he tried to dodge the end of the morning star to his head. His right hand and arm hurt from the weapon.

Sarrjel moved out of the way from the swing of Malicious' blade and struck the demon in the face with her fist. She quickly moved herself out of the way before Malicious could hit her. Suddenly, something flew through the air and missed her head and blew off Malicious' right arm. The demon unleashed a huge scream in pain as he fell to his knees.

"Nephilim's fire your machine guns to strike that bitch!" exclaimed Malicious.

Sarrjel looked through the thick dust of smoke with her special angel sight to see it was Deputy who had fired his bazooka to strike the demon.

Then Sarrjel felt a gust of air and turned to see it was Sarah. Her eyes were pulsing with energy and her sword was raised to fight next to her.

Joe ran as fast as he could through the lawn of the capital with the few militias that were behind him. Johnny saw a huge crowd of demons storming towards them and pulled out his flame thrower gun and pulled the trigger to unleash a huge twenty foot stream of fire. The demons screamed in pain and rolled around along the ground, but then a hell hound jumped over the heap of fire and bodies of demons and attacked Johnny by biting his leg. Johnny screamed in pain just as Irina screamed and pointed her gun but didn't fire. She didn't want to risk hitting him. Champ turned his head quickly who was behind Joe in pursuit and growled as he ran as fast as he could to attack the hell hound.

Joe pulled out his pistol and pointed it at the beast and was about to fire until something flew at him from behind a trash can. It was an imp demon and it pulled the gun from his hand and clawed his eyes as it snarled. Joe screamed in pain as he tried to get the creature off of him.

The hell hound dis-engaged it's powerful jaw from his leg and turned it's head to look at Champ and growled. Champ started barking aggressively as did the hell hound. It was the same hell hound that attacked Irina in the house and fought with Bear. Irina helped Johnny get up, but it was clear he wasn't going to make it without any help.

"Are you going to be alright?" asked Irina.

"No, I'm in fucken pain," he groaned as he limped with his injured left leg.

Champ charged at the hell hound but was met with the snapping jaw of the beast that followed with a snarl. The hell hound grabbed Champs left leg with it's powerful jaw and crushed it, breaking Champ's bone. The German Shepherd unleashed a cry and a wail as he tried to escape from the hell hound. Johnny watched in terror as the hell hound looked at the German Shepherd and then at the two of them that were helpless.

Joe managed to kill the imp with an eight inch army knife and could see the hell hound walking towards them. It looked like it was smiling at them as it panted and then it started to growl and snarl at them as it licked its lips. All of a sudden, Shadow and Bear ran up from behind Joe and both barked at the hell hound. Bear recognized the beast and bared his teeth. Thunder, Duke and Empire emerged from behind the hell hound and attacked as well. There was a loud commotion of barking, snarling and growling from all the German Shepherds and then there was a loud scream and cry from the hell hound before it laid dead on the ground.

Joe walked over to where the German Shepherds were standing over the dead body of the four legged creature. They wagged their tail and panted as Joe kneeled down with them and looked at the ripped body of the monster.

"We got company!" yelled Dallas to Tim and Brenda.

Tim turned his head just as Brenda did while loading their guns and saw thousands of imp demons flying right at them. They screeched and snarled as they swooped down like miniature dragons, but this time they were carrying weapons in their tiny little hands and bony arms. They were two feet tall with large wings that spanned four or five feet. Just as the last batch had unsuccessfully tried to attack and kill the tower guard this batch was determined to slew their enemy with their curved daggers, swords and spears. Brenda and Tim pointed their machine guns at the flying creatures and began to fire just as Dallas fired his. The trio put up a good suppressing fire to keep the monsters from getting close, but then they were running out of ammunition. When Tim or Brenda put in new magazines, they were leaving Dallas vulnerable to being taken out.

Dallas continued to fire his big M1 brown machine gun and screamed like a wild man as the bullets took down lines of demon imps, one after the other. They split apart like paper as they screamed like children, but then one made it through with a curved dagger and cut Dallas' arm as he fired. Dallas quickly grabbed his machete and hit it as he continued to fire his weapon.

Grant dodged the large demon's morning star and swung his nine inch army knife to hit the creature in the face but missed. The demon laughed at him and swung his weapon quickly , hoping to strike him in the face. Grant dodged it and lunged his army knife into the demon's torso with his right arm and cut him just as the demon grabbed his arm. Grant armed his gauntlet blades on his left arm and tried to ram it into the demon's chest but the demon grabbed it with his right hand. He dropped his morning star onto the ground and wrestled with Grant as he glared into his eyes while hissing and sticking out his tongue to intimidate him. Grant grunted as he pushed with all his strength, suddenly he quickly activated his gauntlet blades on his right hand and let go of his army knife. He slashed the edge of his gauntlet blades into the demon's hand, which caused the demon to lose leverage and gave Grant the strength he needed to cut into the demon's chest with his left hand. Sweat rolled down his forehead and blood dripped from his lip just as he unleashed a scream and cut deep into the creature's chest. He pushed through the rib cage as blood spit out of the demon just as he screamed in pain.

"You are weak!" yelled the demon.

"Fuck you!" yelled Grant as he punched the demon as fast as he could with both gauntlet blades into the demon's skull and heard it scream in pain before dying.

Grant breathed heavily as he took deep breathes and looked around to see smoke around him and the sound of bombs going off. He had no idea where the capital was and had a hard time breathing, but then he suddenly saw shadows in the form of dogs come at him and he grabbed the morning star thinking it was hell hounds. His heart fell beneath him and he exhaled with relief as tears emerged in his eyes when he saw it was Shadow and Bear.

Grant started coughing as he kneeled down and felt the dogs give him licks and kisses with their wet noses as they whined and barked, "there there now, I'll be ok."

"Sara!" yelled Rya as he tried to keep her awake. "Stay with me!"

"No it's ok," she whispered as her eyes began to close and open again and then close halfway.

While Rya was pleading with her and trying to keep her alive, someone was behind him and walking quietly. Rya turned around to see a figure directly in front of him kneeling down with him next to Sara. He was wearing a white hooded cloak with silver and gold designs and when he showed his fingers Rya could see scars on the top of his hands just before his wrists. He opened his hood to reveal himself and Rya immediately recognized him. He had brown eyes and an Arabic skin tone with a beard. The Lord smiled and Rya immediately felt a wave of assurance.

"We got to get the hell out of here!" yelled Tim as he shouted to Dallas and continued to fire his machine gun at the imp demons that were flying at them. Suddenly, the imps stopped pursuing and flew away as a drone flew towards them quickly.

Dallas checked to see how many rounds he had and realized he only had twenty left, "oh shit! Get the hell out!"

It was too late the predator drone fired it's machine gun and he felt something strike him in the leg and shoulders. He was wearing a bullet proof vest, but he didn't know how bad the damage was going to be until he got to the ground. Brenda and Tim got shot as well, but they weren't wearing bullet proof vests. They quickly ran down the entrance back into the building from the roof and left most of their heavy guns and only carried their pistols and semi-automatics with them. When they got bellow ground they heard a big explosion as if there was a bomb that had been unleashed.

The predator drone fired another missile at the entrance, but then moved on to attack and kill the rest of the militias.

Sarah and Sarrjel moved their swords quickly to catch the bullets that would have injured or killed them. Their eyes were glowing white with energy and their wings opened up with different Hughes of blues from the middle section of their wings while purple revealed itself prominent from the inside of the wings. Finally the fire power from the nephilim army and human army of the Ravens became to much as the swords moved on their own as fast as the propeller of an airplane and the the angel's spread their arms and they concentrated their power.

The predator drone flew towards where Joe, Grant, Johnny, Irina and company were and locked onto them with its infrared targeting sensors. It opened fired and the bullets hit the concrete leading up to the group but it was meant with heavy resistance from Diamond Back and his M1 Brown machine gun. Deputy was hidden behind a camper and fired his bazooka at the predator drone and struck it in the belly. Before the drone blew up, it managed to get a couple rounds into Diamond Back's arm and chest. Daryl dropped the gun and fell back and looked like he was going to go into shock. The heavy smoke and dust in the air made it difficult for Joe to see, but he knew where Daryl was and ran to him.

"Easy there," said Joe as he pat him down to see where the bullet had gone through and took a breath with disappointment. "You've been shot in the liver."

"I didn't do enough," stammered Daryl.

"You did a lot!" said Joe. "No you are going to live. Just stay with me!"

"Sir, the giants and the demons are closing in on our position," said Grant.

"Sarrjel and Sarah are holding them off," said Joe.

"Yes, but for how long, how long?" asked Grant.

Joe looked at the M1 machine gun and then back at Grant, "take him closer to the capital, take everyone up there. I'm staying behind."

"Sir that's suicide."

Joe looked at Grant and then at Deputy, "you have your orders."

Grant and Deputy looked at each other, but then turned to the other militia members, Jason, Barry Irina and Johnny. They were joined by Dallas, Tim and Brenda as well as Meredith, George, Baker and about fifteen other militias that had survived. They made a run for it with what they had to the top of the staircase beyond the pillars as Joe stayed behind with the big machine gun.

Joe looked over the machine gun and counted six hundred rounds. He looked through the hazy smoke before him that had the marching Raven Army and the charging demons and flying imps above, drawing near. He was beaten down, tired and had cuts around his eyes from an earlier attack. His arms ached and his back hurt, but he felt his adrenaline kick in again and took a deep breath as he aimed the gun at his vehicles.

Sarah and Sarrjel took heavy hits from the Nephilim Army as they marched closer and closer. The angels looked at each other and nodded, suddenly they're bodies began to change and became ghostly and translucent and immediately a blinding light unleashed as they became something else.

When the bright light subsided the nephilims were shocked to see two giant eyes with eyelashes or ghostly looking orbs that were looking at them. They made a strange hymn noise as something moved around them like a ring. It was white and when one of the eyes charged after the first line up of nephilims they were split in half like a hot knife cutting through butter. The other eye shot something out of it's pupil and disintegrated one of the nephilims in the line up.

"What's going on?" asked the president to Master Scaven.

"They're destroying your army with a metamorphic play," said Master Scaven.

"Well, can you stop them?" asked President Krans.

Master Scaven stood their and watched as the angel eyes moved and fired at the attacking giants, "no. You ordered me to protect you."

President Kran shook his head with dis-satisfaction and looked at General Hex, "send in more predator drones!"

"We don't have any. All our infantry is elsewhere," replied General Hex.

The angel eyes were the diameter of four feet and as they turned so did the iris as they looked at the nephilim army charge forward with heavy gun fire and missiles fired from the next wave. The angel eyes charged forward with the moving blade that moved like a saw blade. The army moved evasively too dodged the blade but were split in half and then suddenly were met by another beam of light that disintegrated two more of the giants.

Joe watched from a distance as he saw the two objects attack the army and was keeping them at bay. He lifted the barrel of the gun and aimed at the campers, Jeeps, trucks and other recreation vehicles. He pulled the trigger and fired at each of them and watched them explode after another. Smoke covered the area and there was gun fire from the nephilim army that were in front of the orb like creatures. Joe took cover and ran from sight.

The angel eyes became bigger in size; ten by ten and fired a beam of light at the nephilim army which disintegrated them. As they grew larger so did the Raven Army, more and more regular sized men in black armored uniform fired their machine guns a the creatures, but were fired upon by a white light from their pupil

Joe ran up the capital steps where the remainder of the militia members were and stopped when he saw a man kneeled down in front of Sara. He was wearing a white cloak and held a wooden staff in his hand. He looked like he was busy trying to heal her wounds and Joe could see he pulled something out of her. She screamed and cried in pain as he did, but then there was silence. Joe saw an eight foot archangel with very short black hair wearing gold and silver armor and a seven foot female archangel with white starlit colored hair, lavender eyes who wore a pure silver colored armor. Both of them had their wings folded back and they looked like capes. They were paying close attention to what the man was doing and did not see Joe.

"Keep still child," whispered Jesus as he took a ripped part of Sara's shirt for Rya to hold. "Keep the pressure on her wound."

"What the hell is going on?" demanded Joe as he held his gun tightly and pointed it at the visitor.

The man turned his head to look at Joe just as the archangels did and rose up with his staff. The militia were quiet and the German Shepherds watched quietly to see how their master would react to the new comers.

"We have come as scheduled to take you home," said the man.

"You're late!" yelled Joe. "Just about all my friends are dead because of you!"

"I apologize, I couldn't get here in time, but I am here now," said the Lord.

"What are you going to do?" demanded Joe.

"Do you not know who I am?" said the man

Joe looked at the man, "Jesus."

"Then you haven't forgotten me. Others that live here have forgotten me and the ways to bring the Kingdom of God into their lives."

Joe dropped his gun to the ground and kneeled down slowly, "I have failed you and shouldn't be here. It was I who displayed my ideals of defying your messengers to go elsewhere."

"Rise," said Jesus. "You do deserve to be here with me and it's because of you that you have made it."

Joe rose up and wiped his eyes from the tears. He wasn't sure if it was because of the dirt or the dust, but all he knew was that it was because he was tired and in pain.

Jesus turned to the two archangels, "Michael, Gabriel take the army and kill anything that is within the pillars of the capital and create a barrier from any attack."

"Yes my lord," replied Archangel Michael as he spread his large wings and took to the air followed by Gabriel.

The militia watched with their jaws dropped in dis-belief and shock as thousands of archangels flew up to the sky from behind to capital buildings. The trumpet blew and the war drums could be heard and the war horn was blown to protect them from the Raven Army.

The angel eyes became much larger and were now twenty feet in diameter. They had fired a much broader beam of light to kill more and more of the invading army. The Raven Army suddenly halted as a creature had swooped down and landed on his feet. He unleashed a loud roar and pulled out his sword with his right hand. He pulled out a red rock that looked like a gem or ruby with his left hand and pointed it at one of the angel eyes and a red beam of light shot at them.

The red beam of light struck the angel eye on the left and it began to fluctuate and lose its form until finally it disappeared and Sarrjel was knocked to the ground. She rose her head up and realized what had happened. Master Scaven then pointed the red rock at the second angel eye and a red beam struck it as well. The angel eye fired a white beam of light at Master Scaven and it struck him in the chest. It burned and Master Scaven squealed in pain, but it quickly diminished and the angel eye lost its form. Sarah was thrust upon the ground and looked around slowly to see the demon look at her.

"How about it, bitch. Your head in my hand, your wings cut from your body and given to the imps to chew on and your black hair made into a wig for another bitch to play snow white in a play."

"I think you're dreaming," said Sarrjel.

"You would still have me to tend to, fool," said Sarah.

"I would make you watch and then I would take you as prisoner to be tortured and constantly ridiculed, harassed, laughed at and your wings to be picked apart by vultures as you watch every man, woman and child live in agony, cry and burn alive. Over and over again and you'll get so sick of looking at it you'll claw your own eyes out," laughed Master Scaven as he pulled out his sword.

"Now which of you want to fuck with me?" he yelled in a serious tone

The angels rose up and held their swords in their hand. They circled around him and then unexpectedly Master Scaven wailed on both of them. He moved quickly with his sword against Sarrjel and tried to strike her down, but Sarrjel held her own. Sarah raised her sword and tried to strike the demon from behind but his blade caught hers and he quickly kicked her in the abdomen with his foot. He took advantage of the moment while she was adjusting to the pain and clawed her face with a quick swipe of his talons. Sarah screamed in pain and dropped her sword to reach for her face, which felt like venom was burning her cheeks.

The army of archangels flew through the air with bows and arrows and fired at the imps and larger demons that were charging at them in the air. They moved with grace and speed as though they had done this type of battle more times than they could count. Archangel Michael walked through the rubble of burning vehicles with Gabriel at his side. They were looking for the guardian angels and fought against any stray demons that were charging by foot. The nephilims that fired their missile launchers were charging at Michael and Gabriel with their machine guns that they had picked up from the dead. Michael and Gabriel spun their swords to hit the bullets and caused them to back fire at the giants and killed them. The archer angels had chased away the imps and the demons out of the perimeter of the capital. They flew to the ground with the archangel army and took formation to surround the capital.

Michael looked ahead to see Sarrjel fighting Master Scaven. He looked at Gabriel and pointed for her to take position using hand signals. Gabriel looked at the general and nodded as she took to the air as fast as she could.

Sarrjel swung her sword as fast as she could, but each time she tried to cut him he was always a step ahead. Her right arm hurt from a cut he made and she was distracted by Sarah who was sitting the fight out because she couldn't see and was suffering from being clawed in the face.

"All you have to do is end it with your head, you fucken, dumb cunt!" yelled Master Scaven as he made a move in, by pushing her sword down with his and punched her in the chest as hard as he could and then upper cut her below her chin. Immediately, she dropped her sword and began coughing. Master Scaven then grabbed Sarrjel's sword and stood in front of her as she was on her knees coughing and trying to catch her breath. Then he grabbed the blade with his left hand

and held the handle with his right. Suddenly, the sword began to heat up and turn reddish orange. The handle broke and the demon grabbed the unbreakable blade and bent it into a circle then he quickly put it around Sarrjel's neck. Sarrjel opened her eyes and her mouth in complete chaos as she felt the intense heat around her neck. She unleashed a scream unlike any angel had ever been able to exhale from her lungs.

"Exhale every breath of life before I remove it with my sword," said Master Scaven as he showed the angel his blade and touched it with his fingers. He was just about to decapitate her head when suddenly he heard his name.

"Let her go or I'll have your head!"

Master Scaven turned his head just as Sarrjel turned her eyes to see it was Archangel Michael walking towards him through the smoke and dust. Archangel Micheal looked adamant and pulled out his sword.

"Leave while you still have a chance," ordered Michael.

"How about I leave with these two bitch servants to your Father so I can have Sarrjel's head and torture the other one in the Hole?" asked Master Scaven.

"You're not taking anyone anywhere," commanded Michael as he looked above to see Gabriel waiting for the signal.

Master Scaven looked at Michael with disgust and anger. He knew he couldn't beat him and scoffed at Michael as he grabbed Sarrjel's burning sword that was wrapped around her neck and removed it. He threw it on the ground and lifted her up to her feet.

"You have a good day, Michael. I guess I'll have to wait for vengeance when it is best served cold," yelled Master Scaven as he pushed Sarrjel as hard as he could at Michael and flew away.

"Hey where are you going?" demanded the president.

Master Scaven looked at President Krans and landed in front of him, "I'm leaving to go home, this mission to kill the militia has failed and I can't kill Michael and his army by myself. So I'm leaving."

"But your duty is to protect me," said the president.

"You still have your general and a little bit of your army, fuck you and your protection. I serve the darkness of the light, the Master. Not some piece of shit in a suit," said Master Scaven and he flew away.

President Krans was flustered and looked at General Hex, "mobilize our army to start invading to the capital."

"Start formation, draw your weapons and begin marching in flanks," yelled General Hex.

"Are you alright," asked Michael as he walked over to Sarrjel.

"I think so," said Sarrjel as she touched the burn mark around her neck. It was red and when she touched it, she stammered in cries.

Michael signaled for Gabriel to come down and as she slowly came down she could see the Raven Army marching towards them. Gabriel glided down to the ground with grace and walked over to the two guardian angels.

Sarrjel nodded her head to Michael, Gabriel and Sarah, "I think I'll be fine."

"Sarah your a sight for sore eyes," said Gabriel.

"I'm feeling better, now that you are here. I closed my eyes as I moved my head just as he mauled my face, but the deep scratches will heal," said Sarah.

Archangel Michael looked around to see that the dust had settled and the fires on the burning cars was diminishing. Jesus was walking towards them with two archangels behind Him while the other archangels stood in there lines like concrete statues, ready to draw their weapons.

"Sir, the battle has been won," said Michael.

"Has it now?" asked Jesus as he saw the Raven Army marching towards them.

In front of the army was the President of the United States, the general and two of the Illuminati men and an army of about two-hundred men wearing black armor riot gear with kevlar and black helmets with tinted visors were marching towards them. They held in their hands large machine guns and a huge assortment of weapons on their belts.

"The war is over and they are no match for us, but yet they come," said Gabriel.

"I'll handle this. Uriel, Ariel stay here," ordered Jesus as he walked past Michael and stopped ten feet from the president and the army.

The president stopped his army and walked over to meet with the man that the president saw as a stranger. General Hex walked with him fearing it may be a trick.

"Hello," said President Kran. "We seem to have a miss-understanding. You're harboring terrorist and any man who takes in terrorist is an enemy of the state."

"I'm not a man. I'm the King, King of Kings," said Jesus. "You have no authority over my people."

"I think you're confused, you look like a hippy wearing a bath robe," mocked the president as he began laughing. "We don't have kings here in the real world."

"A wise man once said that one who judges another based on his appearances shall also be judged. Just as all men are judged in the white throne so shall you."

"What?" asked the president confused. "You think you're in charge and you can give me the orders?"

Jesus didn't say anything and could tell President Kran was becoming hostile. He held his staff gently in his right hand and smiled at the man.

"I own the land, the people and everything in this country and there is nothing you can do about it."

"Not past this line," said Jesus as he took the staff and marked the ground with a line. "No man bearing the mark who does not know my face and my name shall cross this line and enter into the Kingdom of God, the paradise that man has created for himself," said the Lord as he commanded and dropped his staff behind him and showed the president and the army, the palm of his hands.

"You're a fool," said the president as he started laughing at Him and he turned to General Hex. "Shoot this idiot and let's continue the march. I want the militia to answer for their crimes."

"Prepare to open fire," yelled General Hex, but he noticed right away that the men in the front lines weren't raising their weapons. Jesus looked at them with an expression of disappointment and sadness. Suddenly, many of the men in the armor stepped forward towards the King of Kings to touch him. They took off their armor and helmets to reveal they were regular people of different races. They had been awakened from deep training and hypnosis to serve the state. They were stopped by an invisible barrier that had been activated as soon as Jesus drew the line in the soil.

"Let me join you, I give you my word I will serve you," said one of the army officers as he had his hand spread on the barrier. Sarrjel and Sarah could see the mark of the beast on his right hand. It was the symbol of a raven with its wings spread apart holding six serpents in its talons, the six serpents which stood for six, six, six.

"I'm sorry my son. I can't save you. You have already made your choice and a dark path it is," said Jesus.

Suddenly, the barrier was overtaken by ten to twenty men banging on the barrier for help and forgiveness. Some of them were crying, shouting angrily and even shooting the barrier to get in.

"Let us in!" they yelled one after the other like crack addicts or spoiled children.

"Let me in!" yelled the president as he walked over to the barrier and placed his hands on it. "Whatever property you think you own, is actually owned by the state. You can not own it. You did not earn it!"

Jesus turned to walk away, he picked up his staff and looked at Sarrjel and Sarah, "come, it's time to go home."

"Will he make it?" asked Joe to Mr. Baker.

"He needs a hospital. He took a bullet in the chest and the blood is black."

Rya looked at Sara as she laid on the concrete breathing, trying to stay alive, "what do you think happens if we die and Jesus is already here?"

"I don't know, but I still don't want you to die," said Rya.

Sara began to laugh, "you've only known me for a few weeks."

Rya started smiling, "yeah I know, but it feels like a lot longer. Just promise me you'll stay with me for the next few minutes."

"Ok," she replied.

Just then Jesus walked over to the crowd of the militia with Michael, Gabriel, Uriel, Ariel, Sarrjel and Sarah. Rya saw his two guardian angels and was shocked to see what had happened to them.

"You are all safe and we're going home," announced Jesus.

"Home?" asked Joe. "More than half of my militia are dead. How are they going to be justified?"

"I realize that," began Jesus. "They are here in spirit and they will be searched by messengers and escorted to heaven where they can be spiritually healed and brought to terms of their death before they can be with their loved ones."

"I thought we were going to Heaven?" asked Joe.

"You are going home, which is where you belong. Heaven is vast and you can spend eternity traveling it," said Jesus.

"Can you heal Diamond Back and my injured?"

"Yes," said Jesus as he walked over to Darryl who was lying on the ground.

He removed the bleeding cloths and stuck his finger in the wound. Darryl screamed in pain and moved his head back and forth.

"What the fuck are you doing?" he yelled.

Jesus pulled the bullet from the wound and covered the wound again with the cloth, "now I need you to close your eyes and believe the wound is gone and that every thing that is worth living for is in the palm of your hand."

A few minutes went by and Darryl kept his eyes closed and took deep breaths. He heard the whispers in Arabic coming from Jesus and suddenly he felt a warm feeling over the wound and a strange tingling sensation over his feet and legs.

Darryl opened his eyes and rose up and took the cloth off of his chest and realized the wound had healed. He looked at Jesus who stood over him with a smile.

"The healing is the first step we go through together, getting over the pain mentally and spiritually we'll take together," Jesus said emotionally as he took Daryl's hand and helped him up.

Joe looked at Jesus in shock, "how did you do that?"

Jesus began to laugh, "nothing will be kept from you and all will be revealed in time."

Jesus walked over to Sara who was also near death and did the same thing that he did for Darryl. When she came to, she began crying and hugged him.

"All is well and you still have strength," said Jesus as he moved on to Johnny who had been bitten by a hell hound and his leg was getting infected from the venom.

Johnny unleashed a huge scream in pain after Jesus had used his staff to pull the venom out like a magnet pulling shrapnel.

After a few minutes had passed since the last healed patient Jesus walked over to his new found friends like a shepherd watching over his sheep. Many of the militia were still in shock over what he could do.

"Now my friends, I know you have many questions and they will be answered. This place you have been living in isn't your home. It is an insulation or testing if you will, to bring back what you have learned to what you already know. It is a prison for Satan and his fallen angels."

"Then why even send us here in the first place?" asked Joe.

Jesus looked at Joe, "you asked to come here. We didn't send you here."

"Wait a minute what?" asked Deputy. "Why the fuck would I want to live in this shit hole?"

"A wise man meets a fool and the wise man is planting his garden and the fool asks him why he doesn't just go to the market to buy food. The wise man says because he doesn't want to spend money on a little when he can work hard once and have a lot. Then the fool says that you'll have to replant the garden after the harvest in the spring. The wise man says that he will have the seeds but the market may not be there tomorrow. Sure enough the cold nights came and after the harvest the market closed and the fool had nothing to eat and begged people off the streets for food."

"Did the wise man help the fool?" asked Irina.

Jesus looked at Irina and smiled, "of course he did and the following spring the fool became a wise man and planted his own garden."

"What has this got to do with us coming here?" asked Joe.

"Yeah," began Deputy. "Why would I give up my old life of living on the beach with my martini and a sexy girl in a bikini?"

Jesus started laughing at Deputy as did the angels, "You chose to live here without your techniques and mind abilities. To create a society that would mirror your own destinies and realities without any help. Men who can create great societies and cities can become great. A woman who can help create the perfect home and family can truly create a miracle."

"Well then what happen? asked Jason.

"Every man has their own vision of the qua or Kingdom of God and not everyone is able to fit into it," said Jesus as he continued. "When you decided to come here you are told that you will lose all your memory of what you have accumulated from your other life your celestial life. When you return home, those memories return to you."

There was a moment of silence and Rya and Sara looked at each other with affection and as she reached for him with her right hand and he took it with his. The militia looked at each other and then at Jesus.

"When do we get to go home?" asked Joe.

Jesus looked at Joe and smiled, "I thought you would never ask. First I need everyone to close their eyes and concentrate on the force field, can you see it?"

At first there was no answer and some of the militias said that they were seeing nothing. Jesus walked around each member of the militia who were either standing up or sitting cross legged.

"Concentrate on the sound of my voice. You're going to go home, but before you do. You need to see where you are and where the invisible barrier is. It should appear as a dome over the capital and it is protecting you from the demons and the Raven Army that are standing by it. Can you see it?"

"I see it," said Irina excitedly.

"Me to," said Barry.

"I'm up in the sky, how do I get down?" asked Dallas.

"Be at ease, you won't fall down," said Jesus. "Master Dallas, concentrate on the ground and you will be there."

"Oh, ok. I'm on the ground. It scared me for a second there," replied Dallas.

"What you are all experiencing is ghost mirroring application. You are all inside the barrier I want you to rip apart the surface."

"Uh, this is going to take all day," said Brenda. "Can't we take a short cut and just open a door?"

"Patience," said Jesus. "Everything has order and we must follow it."

The militia used the ghost mirroring application to remove the surface of the barrier from the inside which revealed a prism color. What would have taken days to cover was done in minutes and when the militia finished they looked around to see a strange surface surround them.

"Now that you have finished I want you to open your eyes," commanded Jesus.

The militia opened their eyes and saw the prism colored barrier around them. The women were gasping in shock and the men were quiet and trying to understand how they did it.

"Now we're ready to go home," said Jesus as he took his staff and pointed to the door way of the capital.

The door began to glow gold and Jesus walked over to it. The militia followed with the archangels behind them.

"This door will lead us home and all you have to do is walk through it."

"We would like to go through first," said Rya.

The militia began to chatter amongst themselves as they were trying to figure out who would go next. Joe took the initiative to make it easy on everyone and went first.

When everyone stepped through the door they were surprised to find themselves at the capital in the city of St Paul. There were so many things going on, so much to take in.

"I can remember now," said Sara.

"I remember to," said Rya.

"I kind of wish I never left," said Joe as he smiled.

"So like, I remember my beach front property, but do I have to give up my AK-47?" asked Deputy to Jesus.

Jesus started laughing and when he stopped he responded, "we don't take away your guns here or anywhere. They belong to you, but we do have a very small percentage of murder in this place."

"I thought you said this was Heaven?" asked Johnny.

"This is home, Heaven is out there. If someone commits murder here they are exiled back to where we just left," said Jesus.

"I remember now," said Sara as she looked as Rya.

"Yeah," began Rya as he looked at Sara and then kissed her. "We're married."

"Let's go home," she replied.

Rya finished typing and stopped as he tried to think of what he wanted to call the novel. Then the light bulb went off in his head as he typed in the title; "An Angel's Whisper". It was a huge accomplishment to get it done the long way instead of the short way. He still kept in touch with Joe and Grant, but the rest of the militia disbanded and went there separate ways. Rya and Sara did some traveling on the bullet train which led to the outer reaches of Haven and they got to meet many faces and visit other places in God's Country but when it was over there was only one place Rya and Sara wanted to go and that was home.

Rya walked out to his balcony that overlooked a fifty acre lawn and looked like a golf course. The trees were trimmed, pruned and looked pristine. It was mid-day and things were similar to the world that he had left except things were brighter, fuller and the people were happy.

"Are you coming to bed?" asked Sara.

Rya turned back from the balcony and walked back to climb into bed. He didn't realize that the girl he met just a few weeks ago was his wife of nearly two millennia and everything was still perfect.

The next morning Rya had that same song in his head "It's in my Dreams That I See Her", and felt Sara's lips on the back of his neck and heard her whisper in his ear, "I love you."

It was at that moment he knew everything was going to be perfect and he didn't want to leave.

The End

Production Notes:

"An Angel's Whisper" is a fantasy novella based on the short story with the same name on "The Legacy Anthology". After publishing "Blue Dragon Fantasy: Fadded Memories and Short Stories". The author decided that he wanted to expand on the 20 page short story by bringing in new characters in the militia and creating an intriguing beginning instead of two main characters who meet a group of people that are one dimensional and they go on a journey somewhere. The project quickly went from 20 pages to nearly 100 pages with added suspense from the demons introduction of the German Shepherds and character development from 10 new militia out of the 50 that are talked about. The re-writes took several months as well as the editing. Instead of the book focusing on the two main characters, Rya and Sara. The story follows the militia themselves as they explore their options, which is their goals and their fears.

In 2011 after publishing "The Temple of the Incubus" the author wrote "An Angel's Whisper" as a spin off for "An Angel's Voice". The two stories go together as a unit because in An Angel's Voice the character of Rya writes "An Angel's Whisper" for a girl he is in love with.

An Angel's Whisper Synopsis:

In a secluded area in Nevada the President of the United States, Scientist, two men from the Illuminati and a group of Luciferians find the technology to open a doorway into another dimension. They're excitement to meet a new alien race soon turns sour when they discover that they are demons and fallen angels. Some look beautiful while others look hideous and also crude beasts on four legs appear as well as imp like creatures. The president meets the leader who calls himself the Master. The Master seduces the president and everyone there to promises and riches beyond their wildest dreams. He promises the president the world and the president worships the Master.

Meanwhile Rya is in his room trying to write his book when Sarah and Sarrjel interrupt him. They tell him that he'll get inspiration if he goes to the art fair. Rya reluctantly decides to listen to them and goes to the art fair where he meets a woman who looks identical to Sarah. She looks so much like her she even has the same name. Their friendship blossoms into romance until one day Rya goes outside to a riot and sees a nightmare of creatures and men in black riot gear fighting with the police, civilians as they're being loaded onto buses.

Rya tries to escape and is saved by a man named Joe who is leader of a small militia. When Joe and the militia meet the guardian angels they are looked upon as fallen angels who can't be trusted.

The angels try to persuade them that they are not fallen angels or demons in disguise. They tell them that they are hear to save them from the evil that has been unleashed. After many attempts to ask the militia to come with them to the capital of Minnesota the militia gets ambushed by demons and the attack causes them to realize that the angels were telling them the truth. The angels ask them again to come with them to Minnesota where they will reach salvation and return home, but the militia want to go to Marshfield Wisconsin where the Army and other militia groups are gathering. The decision causes a conflict; which path should they take? The path to Minnesota with the angels into Minnesota by themselves or a path of uncertainty where they will be with their people in Marshfield Wisconsin.

About the author:

 Ryan Keith Johnson grew up in Somerset WI and started writing in grade school. He enjoyed writing stories as assignments and in sixth
grade decided to write a novel. After graduating High School he moved up to Rice Lake to go to college at WITC for Mechanical Design, but decided to return home because he didn't like it. He went to college at Brown Institute for graphic design and animation. He kept his writing ambitions on the back burner, which later ended up becoming "The King's Retribution", "Lion Ascend" and "The Temple of the Incubus"
	After a head on collision and, a few years latter, a motorcycle accident the author decided to publish a huge collection of short stories and compositions with 20 illustrations that were meant to be sent off with his animation to Disney World. He wasn't sure that if he got into another car accident if he was going to be alive and wanted his best work to be known.
	Johnson continues to write and has more work coming into the future. His new books include "Lion Ascend II" , "Demon Slayer" and "The Will of the Wylde". He also is putting together two children's books that will also be published soon.

www.ingramcontent.com/pod-product-compliance
Lightning Source LLC
Chambersburg PA
CBHW070042030726
47506CB00003B/835